W9-BTH-826

"Make Each Day Your Masterpiece *is a gem, featuring the gentle, loving, God-centered wisdom of the ages. This is a great book for getting centered every day in the things that matter most.*"

—Hyrum W. Smith, Vice Chairman, Board of Directors, FranklinCovey

"Michael Lynberg has written a gentle book—inspiring, inviting, and humble. Page after page, Lynberg shares thoughts from the world's most noble thinkers, giving the reader an easy path on the search for wisdom in the midst of the noise of modern life."

—Timothy P. Shriver, President and CEO, The Special Olympics

"Make Each Day Your Masterpiece *is a masterpiece in itself, brimming with wisdom. Read it from cover to cover or randomly pick one of the short topics for your daily consideration. Either way, the book will certainly enrich you life.*"

—Richard Whitely, Author, *The Customer Driven Company*

"If you want your life to be filled with meaning, then don't miss this valuable guide book. It will nourish your soul with the wisdom of the ages: vital principles that are so often forgotten in this day of being well informed but not necessarily well educated. Read, become educated, and create and save your authentic life—your masterpiece."

—Bernie Siegel, M.D., Author, *Love, Medicine and Miracles* and *Prescriptions for Living*

"For its quotations alone, this book should find its way into every home. It's beautifully written, and I expect that it will bring joy to those who read it. That has been my experience."

—Arthur J. Dyck, Saltonstall Professor of Population Ethics, School of Public Health, and Member of the Faculty of Divinity, Harvard University

"Mike Lynberg has created a deeply inspiring yet practical resource for living an authentic and fulfilling life—a life guided by courage, truth, humanity, and love. This powerful book is a treasure that will beckon you to open its pages again and again."

—Gayle Johnson, Director, Corporate and Foundation Relations, Boston University

"Make Each Day Your Masterpiece *can help you clear the daily hurdles and place you on track toward a more effective and passionate adventure in your daily life."*

—Peter V. Ueberroth

"This book skillfully shows you how to master the ultimate art of creating the life you want."

—John Javna, Author, *50 Simple Things You Can Do to Save the Earth*

Make Each Day Your Masterpiece

Practical Wisdom for Living an Exceptional Life

MICHAEL LYNBERG

Andrews McMeel Publishing
Kansas City

 For information, write Andrews McMeel Publishing, an Andrews McMeel Universal company, 4520 Main Street, Kansas City, Missouri 64111.

ISBN # 0-7407-1968-8
01 02 03 04 05 MVP 10 9 8 7 6 5 4 3 2 1

Library of Congress Cataloging-in-Publication Data

Lynberg, Michael.
Make each day your masterpiece : practical wisdom for living an exceptional life / Michael Lynberg.
p. cm.
Includes bibliographical references.
ISBN 0-7407-1968-8 (hardcover)
1. Life. I. Title.

BD431 .L9665 2001

2001035535

Book designed by Nita Norris

For Elizabeth

CONTENTS

Part Two: **The Path with Heart**

ACKNOWLEDGMENTS

Authors have the wonderful opportunity to publicly thank people who have touched their lives and helped them achieve their dreams. In this tradition, I would like to express my heartfelt gratitude to a number of people.

To begin with, I am grateful to my wife, Elizabeth, who makes each day a masterpiece by being a source of joy and light to all who know and love her. Thank you for believing in me and in this book.

I am also grateful to have been blessed with two loving and dedicated parents, Lee and Joanne Lynberg, who did their best to help their children realize their potential and to live happy and productive lives.

Next, I am grateful to John Wooden, whom ESPN recently named "Coach of the Century." Mr. Wooden, whose UCLA basketball teams won an incredible ten NCAA championships in twelve years, has given me permission to use as the title of this book something that is sacred to him. When he was twelve years old, his father, Joshua Wooden, gave him a card on which he had written a simple creed for living a great life. At the top of the card he had written "Seven Things to Do." Number two was "Make Each Day Your Masterpiece." Mr. Wooden has carried this card with him for over seven decades. He has lived by its principles to the best of his ability and taught countless others to do the same. I've always been inspired by Coach John Wooden and the charge to "make each day your masterpiece," and I am honored to be able to use it as the title of this book.

I also wish to thank the many people who have been kind enough to endorse my work. I am especially grateful to M. Scott Peck, author of The Road Less Traveled and many other fine books, who gave me my break by being the first to praise my work and introduce me to an agent. I'm not sure that I would even be published if it hadn't been for his generous support. I'm also indebted to Norman Vincent Peale, Rabbi Harold Kushner, Norman Cousins, Mark Victor Hansen, Helen Brooks, Richard Edler, Patrick Combs, Vicki Robin, Bill Baker, Scott Wahle, and others who have stood by me with their good names—including those who have kindly endorsed this book. Thank you!

We all stand on the shoulders of giants by building on the work of our predecessors. As an author, I am indebted to countless other writers whose books have helped shape who I am. I also owe a debt to centuries of storytellers, and I'm happy to be able to adapt and include dozens of their wise and wonderful folktales, myths, and parables in this book.

Finally, thank you to my agent, Jane Dystel, who is tireless in helping her authors achieve their best. Thank you, too, to my editors at Andrews McMeel: Erin Friedrich, who has given her all to make this a beautiful and exceptional book, and Dorothy O'Brien, who had the vision for formatting my work in a user-friendly style that I hope many readers will find enjoyable and inspiring.

INTRODUCTION

Why I Wrote This Book, and What It Will Do for You

Several years ago, as a young adult, I earnestly sought answers to some of life's most important questions. How can I make the most of this brief and miraculous existence? What is the meaning of success for me? How can I look back, years from now, with the fewest possible regrets?

Living in Los Angeles and working in a relatively fast-track, prestigious job, I saw many people who defined success in material terms. Yet no matter how much money they made or how much they acquired, they always seemed a step behind their desire for more. Some were burdened with debts and stuck in stressful and unfulfilling positions. Some, to paraphrase a proverb, were spending their health trying to acquire wealth, while others were spending their wealth trying to get back their health. There had to be more to a successful life than this, I thought, and I set out to discover what the great writers, artists, philosophers, scientists, and spiritual masters had to say about the subject.

Over the next few years I read hundreds of books by and about some of the most extraordinary people who had ever lived, and I collected boxes full of note cards with penetrating insights and practical ideas that anyone could use to make his or her life a masterpiece. The hard-won wisdom of Tolstoy, Gandhi, Emerson, Thoreau, Einstein, Mother Teresa, Albert Schweitzer, Viktor Frankl, Helen Keller, Martin Luther King, Jr., and many others—people whose success was not always material—transported me to a place I had never been, an incredible mountaintop where the air was fresh and where one could see clearly for great distances. Although I had not set out to write a book myself, I suddenly had something very important to say, a message to deliver. I was certain that the ideas I had discovered would be helpful to others, too, and it became my mission to share them.

Thus were born my first two books, *The Path with Heart* and *The Gift of Giving,* which were published in 1990 and 1991, respectively. I was fortunate that these books touched many lives and were praised in the media and by a number of best-selling authors, including Norman Vincent Peale, Rabbi Harold Kushner, and M. Scott Peck. Eventually, it was suggested that I rework the two books as one volume and divide the material into short, easy-to-read chapters. I've done this, and the result is the book you're reading now, *Make Each Day Your Masterpiece.* I've also added a great deal of new material, mostly in the form of stories and parables that bring the book's principles to life.

Make Each Day Your Masterpiece is about how we each can make an important difference in this world, not only by achieving great things but also by doing "small things with great love," as Mother Teresa endeavored to do. The book is full of golden nuggets of timeless wisdom from some of the most remarkable people who have ever lived. It will not only help you determine what you really want in life, what you were born to experience and do, but also give you powerful ideas and practical strategies for realizing your goals and dreams.

It is my hope that you will devour this book, turning back the corners of pages you want to revisit, highlighting sentences that touch your heart, that spark something lost or forgotten in your soul. I also hope that you enjoy and are emboldened by its over four hundred inspirational quotations and dozens of moving stories and parables.

Most of all, I hope that *Make Each Day Your Masterpiece* gives you an even deeper sense of wonder and excitement for the miracle of being alive. The very fact that you have started reading this book tells me that you feel compelled to make your life something special. Please know, beyond any doubt, that you can do so. If you make each day your masterpiece, if you live with courage and passion and always do your best, then you will make your life a masterpiece, too, much as Van Gogh, Renoir, and Monet created extraordinary works by painting one small brush stroke at a time. Even if you're unhappy with the way you've lived your life so far, even if your canvas is covered with dark and confused colors, know that you can paint over these now, using them as a background, perhaps, but covering them with bright and colorful acts that are worthy of your extraordinary potential.

Your canvas might be the world of business, or you might want to be a better parent, student, teacher, doctor, artist, writer, inventor, or any of dozens of other noble possibilities. I don't know what your calling is, but I hope this book helps you discover and embrace it, and that it leads you to ever higher levels of excellence, fulfillment, and joy.

May God bless you on your journey. May He comfort and guide you in your time of suffering and need, and may He give you wisdom, courage, faith, hope, and love to live the life you have imagined.

Part One

The Gift of Giving

1
THE PARABLE OF THE TALENTS

Hide not your talents; they for use were made.
Benjamin Franklin

In the Gospel of Matthew, Jesus tells a story about a wealthy man who is about to leave home on a trip. Before departing, the man calls his servants and entrusts his property to them. He gives to each according to his ability: to one he gives five talents (a talent at the time being a measure of silver or currency), to the second he gives two talents, and to the third, one talent. Then he sets out on his journey.

The servant who receives five talents promptly goes and trades with them and makes five more. The servant who receives two talents makes two more in the same way. But the man who receives one talent goes off and digs a hole in the ground and hides what his master has given him.

Some time later, the master of these servants returns and goes through his accounts with them. The man who received five talents comes forward bringing five more. "Sir," he says, "you entrusted me with five talents; here are five more that I have made." "Well done," says the master. "You have shown that you are trustworthy in handling small things; so now I will trust you with greater. Come and share in my happiness." Next, the servant who was given two talents comes forward. "Sir," he says, "you entrusted me with two talents, here are two more that I have made." The master is pleased: "Well done, good servant. You have shown yourself trustworthy in small things; now I will trust you with greater. Come and share in my happiness." Last comes forward the man who was given the single talent. "Sir," he says, "I had heard that you are a hard man, and I was afraid. So I went off and hid your talent in the ground. Look. Here it is. It was yours, now you can have it back." But his master answers him, "You wicked and lazy servant! So you knew that I was a hard man? Well then, you should have at least used your talent to earn interest. So now, take the talent away from him and give it to one who has ten talents. For to everyone who has, more will be given, and he will have more than enough. But the person who has not will be deprived even of what he has. As for this useless servant, throw him outside into the darkness!"

Like many stories in the Bible, the Parable of the Talents holds important truths on how we can best live our lives, on what we can do to make our existence meaningful and fulfilling. Many biblical scholars interpret this parable as meaning that God, like the master in the story, has given each of us certain unique talents and abilities (in fact, it's said that the word "talent" as we use it today has its origin in this story). To live well, we must make use of these special abilities; in fact, we not only must use them, but we also should make them grow. How much or what kind of talents we are given is not important; like the servants in the parable, we are each given different talents and in different measure. What is important is that we use them and expand upon them. Hiding our talents, being lazy, or burying them in fear under a pile of other concerns is a sin against God and against life. It is better to try and lose than to not try at all.

I learned at least this by my experiments:
That if one advances confidently in the direction of his dreams
and endeavors to live the life which he has imagined,
he will meet with a success unexpected in common hours.

Henry David Thoreau

Two roads diverged in a wood,
and I—I took the one less traveled by,
And that has made all the difference.

Robert Frost

One can never consent to creep when one feels an impulse to soar.

Helen Keller

A loving heart is the truest wisdom.

Charles Dickens

God loves the world through us.

Mother Teresa

2
MAKE EACH DAY YOUR MASTERPIECE

There are only two ways to live your life: one is as if everything is a miracle, the other is as though nothing is a miracle.

Albert Einstein

Each person born into this world represents a force, an energy, a promise that has never occurred before and that will never occur again. Only one being like you, with your blend of characteristics and potentialities, will exist in eternity. Only one being like you, with your dreams and aspirations, with your wisdom and experience, born sometimes of joy but often of sorrow and pain, can ever be. In this lies a profound and challenging realization. If you do not live your life completely, realizing values and goals that you hold to be worthwhile, making your unique contribution to the world in which you live, nobody ever will. Your song will die with you.

The moments of our lives, fleeting and irreplaceable, are opportunities to experience the wonders of existence, to "live deep and suck out all the marrow of life," as Thoreau endeavored to do. These opportunities are taken or lost forever. Likewise, the moments of our lives are opportunities to use and develop our special talents and abilities, to do the best we can, with what we have, where we are, and thus to give something back, in gratitude and faith, for the gift of living.

Each of us has a certain style and spirit that we can bring to our daily responsibilities and relationships, ennobling the place where we stand by expressing what is highest in our nature. In this way, anything we do, from sweeping the floor to mending a fence, from caring for our children to helping a stranger in need, is challenging and significant and can make use of our unique blend of talents and abilities. Wherever we are, whatever we do, we can strive to do it well, to express our vision of excellence, thereby expanding our talents and making our part of the world more truthful, beautiful, and caring.

Our daily tasks and responsibilities may seem petty and insignificant, but they are the small brush strokes that together form a living canvas, with all the rich colors and compelling textures that ultimately will make our lives a masterpiece.

When love and skill work together, expect a masterpiece.

John Ruskin

The noblest question in the world is, "What good may I do in it?"

Benjamin Franklin

Nothing can make our life, or the lives of other people,
more beautiful than perpetual kindness.

Leo Tolstoy

Pursue some path, however narrow and crooked,
in which you can walk with love and reverence.

Henry David Thoreau

Live your life while you have it.
Life is a splendid gift—there is nothing small about it.

Florence Nightingale

3
DISCOVER YOUR LIFE'S PURPOSE

Wherever God has put you, that is your vocation.
It is not what we do but how much love we put into it that counts.
Mother Teresa

Some of us are not sure what we want to do with our lives. Perhaps we feel that we do not have any talents worth developing; perhaps, in comparison to others, we feel ourselves to be inferior or inadequately prepared. But everybody has something to give, if only in kindness to one other being, if only in reverence to one small part of creation. In this lies the way to a life of greater meaning and purpose, to discovering and developing what is best in ourselves.

"Everybody can be great," said Martin Luther King, Jr., "because anybody can serve. You don't have to have a college degree to serve. You don't have to make your subject and your verb agree to serve. You don't have to know about Plato and Aristotle to serve. You don't have to know about Einstein's theory of relativity to serve. . . . You only need a heart full of grace. A soul generated by love."

Even if you feel that you do not have any special gifts or

talents, and even if you believe that you are not prepared or powerful enough to make a difference, still you can do something extraordinary with your life. You have only to turn to the holy books of your faith tradition to find examples of courage and compassion. If you are a Christian, you have only to turn to the example of Jesus, asking yourself, as often as possible, "What would he do if he were in my place?" This will elevate your life and give you a sense of purpose "unimagined in common hours."

The important thing is to keep your faith and hope alive, knowing that you are called to do something special with the gift of life; the important thing is to give your best to each challenge and opportunity that comes your way. "Do not waste life in doubts and fears," advised Ralph Waldo Emerson. "Spend yourself on the work before you, well assured that the right performance of this hour's duties will be the best preparation for the hours or ages that follow it."

In fulfilling the work before us, in striving to do our best at everything we do, we come to discover ourselves and our true abilities. Self-knowledge, awareness of our unique gifts and potentialities, does not come solely from introspection, from thinking about what we are meant to do in life, but from testing ourselves against the world in which we live. "How can we learn to know ourselves?" asked Goethe. "Never by reflection, but by action. Try to do your duty and you will soon find out what you are."

It is best, even if we are not sure what we want to do with our lives, to stay active, to make the most of the opportunities before us. In this way, we can test our limits, learn from our mistakes, and adjust our course; in this way, our talents will reveal themselves. Furthermore, in fulfilling the work before us, we will grow in our capacity to do more. "The reward for doing one duty is the power to do another," says the Talmud.

Do not lose heart, even if you must wait before finding the right thing, even if you must make several attempts. Be prepared for disappointment, but do not abandon your quest.

Albert Schweitzer

To lose your way is one way of finding it.

African Proverb (Swahili)

I am only one, but still I am one. I cannot do everything, but still I can do something.

Helen Keller

It is our duty as men and women to proceed
as though the limits to our abilities do not exist.
Pierre Teilhard de Chardin

Once I asked my confessor for advice about my vocation.
I asked, "How can I know if God is calling me
and for what He is calling me?"
He answered, "You will know by your happiness.
If you are happy with the idea that God calls you to serve Him
and your neighbor, this will be the proof of your vocation.
Profound joy of the heart is like a magnet
that indicates the path of life. One has to follow it,
even though one enters into a way full of difficulties."
Mother Teresa

4
BE TRUE TO YOUR CALLING

Many persons have a wrong idea of what constitutes true happiness.
It is not attained through self-gratification,
but through fidelity to a worthy purpose.
Helen Keller

While some are still searching, others among us have a compelling sense of what we want to do with our lives. We have a vision, a purpose that resonates to the very core of our being. Somehow we know that our lives will never be complete unless we answer this calling. A part of us, that part which is most precious and unique, will always remain unfulfilled unless we find the courage and determination to step out from the crowd and be different, to live up to the standards of our heart rather than to the expectations of those around us.

Some of us, for example, are blessed with a special dream or vision, a cherished idea that we feel compelled to bring forth from our imagination and into reality. Perhaps we have a talent for invention and have thought of a certain product or service, or the improvement of an existing one, that could bring comfort or joy into the lives of others; perhaps we have thought of a way to alleviate some of the world's terrible suffering. "Some men see things as they are and say why?" said the poet Robert Frost. "I dream of things that never were and say why not?" Giving birth to your idea, feeding and caring for it, carefully dressing it and bringing it into the world, loving it even when it sometimes rejects your best efforts, may be the expression of your highest talents.

Others among us are gifted with a certain skill or ability, for teaching, for example, or for medicine, nursing, or scientific research, at which we may truly excel and make a contribution. To make use of our talents, to follow our heart in this direction, we may have to forgo an easier, more immediately rewarding path and go through many years of difficult study and rigorous training. Perhaps our research will take us to the far reaches of the globe or keep us many nights in the world of our laboratory; perhaps our desire to help others will lead us away from comfort and security and into the hard world of the poor and destitute. Though enriching the lives of others may never make you rich in a material sense, you will gain another kind of riches by expressing your highest talents, pursuing your dreams, and making a difference in the world.

Many of us may feel that our talents and abilities call us to be a part of a business or organization in which we can work with others toward some common, worthwhile goal. Perhaps we have an interest in computers, for example, or in broadcasting, publishing, aviation, or public service. Maybe our talents are highly specialized or lie in coordinating, marketing, or selling the products and services of others. There are many things that require the concerted efforts of a number of individuals, each fulfilling his or her unique capabilities. In working together, we are able to accomplish more than any could accomplish alone; in harmony with others, our song may become an elegant concerto or a powerful symphony.

Some of us are called to more vigorous and physical pursuits, combining the love in our hearts with the strength in our arms to cultivate the earth, to harvest grain, or to fashion this grain into the bread that we eat. Or perhaps we like to build things, to blend intelligence with skill to create homes, roads, bridges, ships, hospitals, universities—any of the thousands of things that make our lives safer, more comfortable and enriching. Or maybe we like to fix and repair what has already been built, believing that it is good to conserve and make last, rather than to throw away, which has become so easy and prevalent in our world.

Still others are called to do the most important work of all—raising children: loving them, caring for them; helping them to savor life in all its splendor and complexity; teaching them, by our example, virtues like courage, faith, honesty, and kindness, so that they might take their place in the chain of life and make their unique contribution to the world. A child is God's greatest gift; raising a child is life's most solemn and joyful responsibility.

Then there are those drawn to the arts, who are, as Aleksandr Solzhenitsyn remarked in his Nobel Prize address, "given to sense more keenly than others the harmony of the world and all the beauty and savagery of man's contribution to it—and to communicate this poignantly to people." In your heart you may wish to be a painter, actor, writer, dancer, or musician. You may be willing to give your life for your art, to sacrifice everything for creative excellence, beauty, and truth. This sacrifice may be necessary, for the life of the artist, while full of adventure and the thrill of creativity and discovery, can also be lonely and without the rewards valued by much of society. "Perhaps it will turn out that you are called to be an artist," wrote Rainer Marie Rilke in his *Letters to a Young Poet.* "Then take that destiny upon yourself and bear it, its burden and its greatness, without asking what recompense might come from the outside. For the creator must be a world for himself." And Carl Jung observed that it is sometimes necessary for the artist, in developing his talents and giving expression to his art, "to sacrifice happiness and everything that makes life worth living for the ordinary human being."

No matter where we are in life, whether we are parents doing the most important work of all, or whether we have the freedom and inclination to pursue a special dream, all of us have unique gifts and talents that must be discovered and developed, explored and expressed, if we are to live our lives fully. Following our hearts, doing work that we love, will draw out our most noble qualities and become our most valuable gift to the world in which we live.

God could not be everywhere and so He made mothers.

Jewish Proverb

Choose a job you love
and you'll never have to work a day in your life.

Chinese Proverb

I'll walk where my own nature would be leading;
it vexes me to choose another guide.

Emily Brontë

A musician must make his music, an artist must paint,
a poet must write if he is to ultimately be at peace with himself.
Abraham Maslow

The person who is born with a talent
finds his greatest happiness in using it.
Goethe

5
YOU CAN WEATHER LIFE'S STORMS

Life begins on the other side of despair.

Jean Paul Sartre

Many of us remain a stranger to what is highest and most noble in our nature. Sometimes this is not our fault; we would like to move forward, but we have been injured by the harshness of life, and we are, for the moment at least, unable to answer our calling. Perhaps we have lost something of value—a loved one, our health, a dream, or an ideal—and there is a dark emptiness, a bewildering vacuum, that we are struggling to understand and fill. Or perhaps our hearts were wounded by betrayal—someone used us without thought or sympathy, or for blatantly selfish ends—and we are frozen with pain and unable to move ahead as we would like.

We will deal with loss and despair at considerable length later in this book. For the moment, however, know that with time, patience, and some effort, most of us will recover. We will never again be the same—we will always be painfully aware of our essential vulnerability, of how our lives can turn on a dime—but we will once again be able to enjoy life and to pursue dreams and ideals that give our existence meaning.

"Providence has a thousand ways of raising up the fallen, succoring the weary," wrote Goethe. "Our destiny sometimes has the appearance of a fruit tree in the winter. Looking at its dreary aspect, who would think that these stiff branches, these jagged twigs, will turn green again and bloom next spring and then bear fruit. Yet this we hope, this we know."

As the author of Ecclesiastes expressed,

To everything there is a season
And a time for every purpose under heaven:
A time to be born and a time to die
A time to plant and a time to uproot. . . .
A time to tear down and a time to build
A time to weep and a time to laugh
A time to mourn and a time to dance.

If this is your season of mourning and weeping, if something in your life has been torn down and uprooted, then first and foremost, be gentle and patient with yourself, as you would with a friend. Beyond this, realize that you can gain strength by turning to God, who waits to help you, and by asking for His comfort and guidance in enduring your loss. In this sense, the Parable of the Talents has an even deeper meaning, for it also applies to our spiritual growth. As we turn to God and ask for His help in growing in faith, hope, love, patience, kindness, forgiveness, perseverance, and other virtues, we find that these gifts multiply. Though nothing can replace our loss, we can know a sense of peace and consolation.

Finally, for the moment, before we deal with these issues in greater depth, know that you are not alone in your suffering. According to an ancient tale from China, a woman once went to a holy man and asked for his help in enduring a terrible loss. "What prayers, what magical incantations do you have to help me?" she asked.

The holy man listened to her story and said, "Go and find a mustard seed at a house that has never been touched by sorrow. Bring it to me, and we will use it to help end your suffering."

So the woman went forth and came to one of the most beautiful houses in the city. Surely these people have known nothing but good fortune, she thought, and she knocked on the door. An elderly couple asked her to come in.

"Can you please help me," said the woman. "I am trying to find a home that has never been touched by sorrow. It is very important."

The elderly couple said, "We are sorry. You have come to the wrong place," and they began to tell her about the tragic things that had happened in their lives.

The woman felt compassion for them, and she tried to comfort them; for a time, this made her forget about her own troubles.

Then she went out again and searched for a home that had never been touched by sorrow. She went to all parts of the city, visiting people in poor hovels and rich mansions. She heard tale after tale of sadness and loss, and all the while she comforted the weary and consoled the afflicted. As she did this, her own suffering became more distant, and she realized that her quest for the mustard seed had succeeded at driving some of the sorrow from her life.

There is no grief which time does not lessen and soften.

Cicero

When sorrows come, they come not as single spies, but in battalions!

William Shakespeare

I have been driven many times to my knees
by the overwhelming conviction that I had nowhere else to go.
My own wisdom and that of all about me
seemed insufficient for the day.

Abraham Lincoln

Even in the deepest sinking
there is the hidden purpose of an ultimate rising.
Thus it is for men; from none is the source of light withheld
unless he himself withdraws from it.
Therefore the most important thing is not to despair.

Hasidic Saying

Providence always comes to our help.
When the need is immediate,
the intervention of Providence is also immediate.
It is not always a matter of huge amounts,
but of what is needed at a given moment.

Mother Teresa

6
DO THIS –
AND YOU'LL NEVER BE BORED AGAIN

I am not bound to win, but I am bound to be true. I am not bound to succeed, but I am bound to live up to what light I have.

Abraham Lincoln

Many of us are not in life's winter; we are capable of developing our talents and pursuing our dreams, yet we sometimes refrain from doing so for other reasons. Perhaps we are paralyzed by fear of the unknown, of stepping out and being different, or of failing at something that we know in our hearts to be worthwhile (it is much less painful to fail at something unimportant). Perhaps we are tied down by the unfair expectations of those around us, or shackled by the false values and shallow ideals that we have mistakenly adopted from the world in which we live.

At moments of inspiration, in the soft glow of a winter's evening by the hearth, or during a solitary spring afternoon walk, we catch a glimpse of the greater life that is possible for us. The "still small voice" whispers a dream or an ideal, and we sense that it can be attained, or at least that its pursuit would be both challenging and fulfilling. But later that day or perhaps the next, our vision starts to fade, and a number of smaller events and exigencies flood in to dominate our time and attention. Immersed as we are in the practical, our dreams and aspirations seem uncertain and perhaps a bit foolish. The path with heart, which winds across lush green meadows, through rolling foothills and up jagged, snow-capped peaks, seems perilous and steep. Although the countryside is rich and beautiful and although the heights are majestic with clear and spectacular vistas, the path itself seems untrodden and dangerous. We could get lost in the woods or fall from a cliff, or perhaps we could succumb to exposure and fatigue. Certainly, if the path were a good one, more would have passed this way before, we think, and we opt for something less dangerous.

The air in the lowlands may be hazy and dense, but we are not without company. Many plod the highway of conformity, each following the other in what no one cares to realize is a closed circle. We seek what others seek: comfort, security, money, power, pleasure. But no matter how much of these we attain, we always seem to yearn for more, and a higher part of our nature remains unfulfilled. We are not alone in our conformity; we are only strangers to our better selves.

Sometimes we are willing to sell our ideals and trade our greater talents for a success that seems more tangible and secure, a success that can be measured in dollars and cents.

Sometimes we are willing to sacrifice a challenging and fulfilling life today in order to hurry for what we hope will be a life of ease and comfort tomorrow. With age, however, we realize that these goals recede before us like a mirage in the desert. Success and happiness are not distant goals that we suddenly capture and hold, they happen incidentally when we are fulfilling ourselves, when we have found our place and are giving of our most cherished abilities.

If we have taken the wrong path, however, years can vanish as we go through our routines, sacrificing the higher part of our nature, our greatest potential for growth and fulfillment, to the trivial urgencies that press upon us from all sides. We may find ourselves talking less and less about our forsaken dreams, talents, and ideals, and there seems to be an unspoken, polite agreement not to trouble others about theirs. The further we get from them, the dimmer they become, until, perhaps, listlessness and boredom set in, and life, to paraphrase Schopenhauer, seems nothing more than the repetition of the same tiresome play. It has been said that years leave wrinkles upon the skin, but this loss of enthusiasm, of passion and ideals, wrinkles the soul. Like the timid servant in Jesus' story, we have been thrown into a world of darkness.

We may earn considerable amounts of money and we may try to fill our lives with many fine ornaments and possessions, but something inside remains empty and craving, a question goes unanswered. For once we attain a certain level of comfort and security, it is natural and uniquely human to long for something higher, a sense of purpose, a pursuit that exercises our most cherished abilities and capacity for service, making us feel a worthwhile part of the world in which we live. If we follow this longing for a higher purpose, our lives will be transformed and become full of passion, growth, and discovery. Our world will be full of possibilities; there will be little time for boredom.

I know of no more encouraging fact than the unquestionable
ability of man to elevate his life by conscious endeavor.
Henry David Thoreau

Every person must feel a responsibility to discover his mission in life.
God has given each normal person a capacity to achieve some end.
Potential powers of creativity are within us,
and we have the duty to work assiduously to discover these powers.
Martin Luther King, Jr.

I have no special revelation of God's will. . . .
He reveals Himself daily to every human being,
but we shut our ears to the "still small voice."

Mahatma Gandhi

Prayer enlarges the heart until it is capable of containing
God's gift of Himself.

Mother Teresa

Prayer is not . . . idle amusement.
understood and applied, it is the most potent instrument of action.

Mahatma Gandhi

7
THE SECRET TO FILLING YOUR LIFE WITH PURPOSE AND MEANING

Believe, when you are most unhappy,
that there is something for you to do in the world.
So long as you can sweeten another's pain, life is not in vain.
Helen Keller

The importance of making the most of our unique gifts and abilities, expressed in the Parable of the Talents in the Gospel of Matthew, is also emphasized in other great world religions, philosophies, and contemporary psychological theories. Judaism, for example, is profoundly concerned with giving life meaning, with working with God to fulfill His plan. Each person plays his or her part: "It is not upon thee to finish the work," it says in the Talmud. "Neither art thou free to abstain from it." Each of us has a unique role to play in this work. "I am a creature of God and my neighbor is also His creature," says another verse in the Talmud; "my work is in the city and his in the field; I rise early to my work and he rises early to his. As he cannot excel in my work, so I cannot excel in his work. Perhaps you say, 'I do great things and he does small things.' But we have learnt that it matters not whether one does much or little if he only directs his heart to Heaven."

Martin Buber, in an inspiring essay on the teachings of Hasidism, a sect of Judaism, writes that each person's "foremost task is the actualization of his unique, unprecedented and never recurring potentialities, and not the repetition of something that another, and be it even the greatest, has already achieved." According to Hasidism, it is through our work and the everyday exercise of our talents that one has access to God. But each person has a different access. "God does not say: 'This way leads to me and that does not,' but he says: 'Whatever you do may be a way to me, provided you do it in such a manner that it leads you to me. . . .' Everyone has in him something precious that is in no one else. But this precious something in a man is revealed to him only if he truly perceives his strongest feeling, his central wish, that in him stirs his inmost being."

Islam, like Judaism and Christianity, the religions from which it springs and which Muslims believe it completes, also stresses that living a good life comes in part through giving of one's uniqueness and individuality. "To each is a goal to which God turns him," says the Koran. "Then strive together as a race toward all that is good." Another verse continues, "When a man dies, they who survive him ask what property he has left behind. The angel who bends over the dying man asks what good deeds he has sent before him." And, "You will never attain righteousness until you give freely of what you love."

In Buddhism, one step in the eightfold path to overcoming life's sufferings and the prison of our own selfishness is through right livelihood. Our work occupies a great deal of our waking attention, and the Buddha considered it impossible to progress spiritually if our occupation pulls us in the opposite direction: "The hand of the dyer is subdued by the dye in which it works." It is therefore imperative that a person get in the right place, a vocation that calls forth his greatest love, that connects him with life around him, and that breaks down the hard shell of his ego and his tendency to be a separate entity living only for himself. This right place is unique to each individual. "Your work is to discover your work," said the Buddha, "and then with all your heart to give yourself to it."

Hinduism, like Buddhism, also stresses the importance of doing good works in a spirit of service and sacrifice. But unlike Buddhism, Hinduism advocates a tradition of castes, a rigid social system in which people fall into one of four general classes or vocations, not according to their individual talents or inclinations but according to the family into which they are born. The caste system led the former prime minister Jawaharlal Nehru to comment that India is "the least tolerant nation in social forms while the most tolerant in the realm of ideas." This may be true, especially since Hinduism is so open to the many different ways or religions by which it believes one may come to know God, and since it is so accepting of where an individual may be in his or her own spiritual quest. ("If we have listening ears, God speaks to us in our own language, whatever that language be," wrote Mahatma Gandhi, a devout Hindu.)

This paradox within Hinduism notwithstanding, one of the four paths, or yogas, by which a Hindu may reach God is Karma Yoga. This path stresses the importance of creative action, the manner or spirit in which one lives and discharges his duties. The work one does is not as important as the way in which one does it. The goal, as in Buddhism, is to transcend the smallness of the finite self, and this is done when a person works with love, without thought for personal gain, and in devotion to God. "Do without attachment the work you have to do," says the Bhagavad Gita, "surrendering all action to Me . . . freeing yourself from longing and selfishness."

By focusing on God and on service, the Karma Yogi is beyond concern for himself: "One to me is loss and gain; one to me is fame or shame; one to me is pleasure, pain." He is serene, focused only on making the work at hand a gift to his beloved God, and this calls out his highest and most noble powers.

That which each can do best, none but his Maker can teach him.

Ralph Waldo Emerson

No limits are set to the ascent of man, and the loftiest precincts are open to all. In this, your choice alone is supreme.

Hasidic Saying

Each of us possesses a Holy Spark,
but not everyone exhibits it to best advantage.
It is like the diamond which cannot cast its luster
if buried in the earth. But when disclosed in its appropriate setting
there is light, as from a diamond, in each of us.

Rabbi Israel of Rizin

Rabbi Baer once said to his teacher, the seer of Lublin:
"Show me one general way to the service of God."
The zaddik replied: "It is impossible to tell men what way they
should take. . . . Everyone should carefully observe what way his
heart draws him to, and then choose this way with all his strength."

Martin Buber

It is better to do your own duty, however imperfectly,
than to assume the duties of another person, however successfully.

The Bhagavad Gita

8
CLEAR YOUR MIND OF "CAN'T"

The person who says it cannot be done
should not interrupt the person doing it.
Chinese Proverb

Those who believe that they cannot make the most of their unique talents and abilities, or that it's not important, should be aware that doing so is called for not only by the world's great religions but also by some of its great philosophies. Confucianism, for example, the great system of thought that for 2,500 years has shaped the character of China and other nations in Asia, also advocates that we express what is best and highest in our nature. "Wherever you go," said Confucius, "go with your whole heart." His greatest disciple, Mencius, wrote, "Those who follow that part of themselves which is great are great; those who follow that part which is little are little."

Like Socrates in Greece, Confucius practiced what he taught and set an example for others to follow. Although poor and often ridiculed, he would not compromise the ideals or principles by which he lived, even if this meant turning down a comfortable position offered by those in power. "With coarse food to eat, water to drink, and my bent arm for a pillow, I still have joy in the midst of these things," he said. "Riches and honors acquired by unrighteousness mean no more to me than floating clouds."

In Western philosophy, Aristotle is the first and foremost advocate of the importance of developing our talents and realizing our highest potential. For Aristotle, humans are animals and, like other animals, they have certain physical needs that must be satisfied: the need for food and safety, for example. But what makes humans unique, what distinguishes them from other forms of life, is their ability to reason and to contemplate. It is this rational capacity that must be developed and realized if we are to live well and be fulfilled. "What is proper to everyone is in its nature best and most pleasant for him," says Aristotle. "The life that accords with reason will be best and most pleasant for man, as a man's reason is in the highest sense himself. This will therefore be also the happiest life."

This is not to say that one has to become a philosopher in order to be happy. Aristotle was open-minded enough to recognize that different people have different intellectual and contemplative interests; for example, a person may be interested in music, medicine, politics, art, construction, or any other profession that requires thought and attention. What is important is that one pursue the subject for which he has the greatest affection, for this will lead to the best results. "It is so too with people who are fond of music or architecture or any other subject; their progress in their particular subject is due to the pleasure which they take in it. Pleasure helps increase activity," and there is an intimate connection between pleasure and the "activity which it perfects."

The American philosopher Ralph Waldo Emerson also stresses the importance of pursuing work in which we have a particular interest and which gives us pleasure. "The high prize of life, the crowning fortune of a man, is to be born with a bias to some pursuit which finds him in employment and happiness." In his essay "Self Reliance," Emerson emphasizes the importance of following one's heart, of developing one's most unique talents and most cherished abilities: "There is a time in every man's education when he arrives at the conviction that envy is ignorance; that imitation is suicide; that he must take himself for better or worse as his portion; that though the wide universe is full of good, no kernel of nourishing corn can come to him but through his toil bestowed on that plot of ground which is given him to till. The power which resides in him is new in nature, and none but he knows what that is which he can do, nor does he know until he has tried."

These philosophers and many others have agreed: No one is on this earth merely to take up space. Each of us has a purpose in life that we must try to discover and express. To do so, we must clear our mind of "can't" and step out from the crowd, fulfilling what is highest in our nature. This may lead to a way full of difficulties, but it will fill our lives with a sense of purpose, joy, and meaning that we can know in no other way.

Our doubts are traitors,
and make us lose the good we oft might win by fearing to attempt.
William Shakespeare

God loves me. I'm not just here to fill a place, just to be a number.
He has chosen me for a purpose, I know it.
He will fulfill it if I don't put an obstacle in his way.
He will not force me. . . . He wants us to say yes.
Mother Teresa

Be watchful, stand firm in your faith, be courageous, be strong.
Let all that you do be done in love.
I Corinthians 16:13–14

Harmony and strength exist in our lives
only when [there is] harmony between our deepest and purest
yearnings and the goals we pursue in life.

Albert Schweitzer

Lord, grant that your love may so fill our lives
that we may count nothing too small to do for you,
nothing too much to give, and nothing too hard to bear.

St. Ignatius Loyola

9
DO THE BEST YOU CAN, WITH WHAT YOU HAVE, WHERE YOU ARE

What you do I cannot do.
What I do you cannot do.
But together you and I can do something beautiful for God.
Mother Teresa

In addition to the world's great religions and philosophies, contemporary psychology is also rich in writings that describe the importance of developing our unique talents and pursuing our highest ideals. Abraham Maslow was a psychologist who devoted his career to studying what he called "peak performers," the small segment of the population that progressively actualizes its talents and capabilities. He discovered a number of important things.

To begin with, Maslow believed that the average person is motivated primarily by deficiencies—by trying to fulfill his most basic needs for food and safety, belongingness and affection, respect and self-esteem—whereas the truly healthy person has satisfied these needs and moved beyond them. According to Maslow, peak performers are focused on developing and realizing their "fullest potentialities and capacities." They have a sense of purpose or mission, and they strive to realize certain values that they hold dear through their work and conduct.

Maslow believed that these higher needs—having a sense of mission and realizing certain values—can be just as important to our well-being as fulfilling the basic needs. If we ignore them, we will never be fulfilled or at peace with ourselves. "If you deliberately plan to be less than you are capable of being," he said, "then I warn you that you'll be unhappy for the rest of your life. You will be evading your own capacities, your own possibilities."

Another extraordinary student of human nature was Viktor Frankl, who survived the horrors of Auschwitz and founded a school of psychotherapy known as logotherapy. Frankl believed that a person's primary motivation is not pleasure, as Freud believed, nor the will to power, as Adler believed (basing his psychology on Nietzsche's ideas), but the *will to meaning*. What people want most, what they are even willing to die for, is for their lives to be meaningful, significant. One of the ways in which people can make their lives meaningful is through work and the manner in which they carry out their tasks and responsibilities.

"With his unique destiny each man stands, so to speak, alone in the entire cosmos," writes Frankl. "His destiny will not recur. No one else has the same potentialities as he, nor will he himself be given them again." The concrete task of each individual is relative to his uniqueness and singularity; "The radius of the activity is not important; important alone is whether he fills the circle of his task."

Mental health, according to Frankl, "is based on a certain degree of tension, the tension between what one has already achieved and what one still ought to accomplish, or the gap between what one is and what one should become." Remarkably, Frankl found, through his dreadful experience as a prisoner in a concentration camp, that this tension can even be a matter of life and death. "In the Nazi concentration camps," he writes, "one could have witnessed that those who knew that there was a task waiting for them to fulfill were most apt to survive." Quoting Nietzsche's aphorism "He who has a why to live for can bear with almost any how," Frankl credits his own survival, particularly with a near fatal bout with typhus fever, to his desire to rewrite a manuscript that the Nazis had confiscated when he entered the camp.

With so many voices of wisdom—the great writers, thinkers, and spiritual leaders of the ages—counseling us to develop our most cherished talents, to express our uniqueness and individuality, and to make our work a gift to God and to the world in which we live, why do so many of us settle for less? To expand on a familiar a metaphor, why are we compelled to linger near the coast, exploring shallow waters, swinging safely at anchor, or sinking our keel into riches and pleasures, when we could set sail for the not-so-distant shores of our greatest potential, for the unexplored lands of our fondest dreams?

Do the best you can, with what you have, where you are.
Theodore Roosevelt

There is as much dignity in tilling a field as in writing a poem.
Booker T. Washington

We can do no great things—only small things with great love.
Mother Teresa

If you have love you will do all things well.
Thomas Merton

I have never had a policy;
I have simply tried to do what seemed best
each day as each day came.
Abraham Lincoln

10
WHAT YOU CAN LEARN FROM CHILDREN THAT WILL MAKE YOU A SUCCESS

Nobody knows what's in him until he tries to pull it out.

Ernest Hemingway

Many of us are aware that a greater life is possible. We sense that we have scarcely realized our potential, our powers, and that there lie vast continents, strange and wonderful worlds of unexplored territory, within. "Compared to what we ought to be," wrote William James, "we are only half awake. Our fires are damped, our drafts are checked, we are making use of only a small part of our mental and physical resources."

In looking back, many of us can remember times when we were rewarded for exploring our talents, for taking risks, either by getting what we wanted or by learning in the process. Everything we can do, all the skills we possess, came from taking chances, from finding the courage to gingerly test the chill waters of the unknown. Learning to walk and talk, to read and write, to understand and get along with others, to cope with our disappointments and losses, discovering our love for music, art, literature, science, or athletics—everything we have accomplished and learned, as individuals and as a race, has come from our willingness to reach beyond ourselves. Without this willingness we would neither have matured nor survived.

Children have a natural inclination to reach beyond themselves, to try new things and to test their limits. Yet as we grow older, we sometimes become afraid of falling down, of appearing foolish or getting hurt. The sorrows and disappointments of life erode our strength as water wears away stone.

Looking around, we see those few unbroken souls who have managed to reach for their dreams, to take risks and explore their most cherished talents and abilities. The scientist who, after many years, makes a startling breakthrough that saves lives or helps us understand our world. The artist who creates a beautiful song, poem, or picture that awakens our soul and makes us grateful to be alive. The athlete who reminds us of the strength, endurance, and remarkable agility of the human body. The innovator who, despite the odds, brings a valuable product or service to market, making us wonder how we ever managed without it. In many cases, these people are rewarded for their excellence—materially, financially, and with recognition from their peers and admiration from others. More important, however, their lives have elements of passion and joy, meaning and fulfillment, that are often lacking in the lives of those who will not or cannot be true to their higher calling.

If I am like others, who will be like me?

Yiddish Proverb

Once you say you 're going to settle for second,
that's what happens to you in life, I find.

John F. Kennedy

Strength does not come from physical capacity.
It comes from an indomitable will.

Mahatma Gandhi

Always bear in mind that your own resolution to succeed
is more important than any one thing.

Abraham Lincoln

to be nobody but yourself—
in a world which is doing its best, night and day,
to make you like everybody else—
means to fight the hardest battle which any human
being can fight, and never stop fighting

e. e. cummings

11
LEAVE YOUR FOOTPRINTS ON THE SANDS OF TIME

Life is what we make it, always has been, always will be.
Grandma Moses

It is tempting to imagine that those who achieve greatness, in whatever measure, within whatever radius of activity, had decisive advantages at the start. We often think that they somehow had means and opportunities that are unavailable to most. But seldom is this true.

Charles Dickens was pulled out of school at the age of twelve to support himself by working in a shoe polish factory while his parents were in debtor's prison.

Grandma Moses spent her life on a farm raising ten children before taking up painting at the age of seventy-eight, when her arthritic hands could no longer hold an embroidery needle; by the time she was ninety, her paintings were known and loved the world over.

Abraham Lincoln walked for miles with legendary resolve just to borrow a book. "I will study and get ready, and perhaps my chance will come," he said.

Hellen Keller lost her sight and hearing as an infant, yet she went on to graduate with honors from Radcliffe, to write several books, to lecture, and to inspire people everywhere not to feel sorry for themselves but to make the most of what they have. "Life is either a daring adventure or nothing," she said

Nor do people who live extraordinary lives necessarily have an easy path. No one rolls stones out of their way; more likely than not, others may even try to block their passage.

Mohandas K. Gandhi was imprisoned numerous times in his struggle to lead India, nonviolently, to independence, and he ultimately died trying to unite the nation when it was being torn apart by sectarian hatred. His countrymen called him "Mahatma," which means "Great Soul."

Martin Luther King, Jr., was repeatedly threatened (along with his wife and children), had his house fire-bombed, was imprisoned nineteen times for standing up nonviolently to unjust laws, but pressed on in love and faith, even when he had an uncanny premonition of his own death.

Albert Schweitzer left a comfortable life as a university professor and parish minister to return to medical school. Upon completion of his studies, at the age of thirty-eight, he traveled to French Equatorial Africa, where he cleared the forest and built a hospital with his bare hands. For over fifty years, he served people who would otherwise have suffered and died of preventable causes.

Mother Teresa also left a relatively comfortable life as a teacher at a Loretto school and convent in Calcutta. At the age of thirty-eight, she took to the streets, alone and with no definite plan of where or how to begin, because she felt called to make God's love manifest in action, serving the poorest of the poor. Those who knew her at Loretto say that they had no idea of her strength and determination; she had always seemed so meek and delicate in comparison to others.

None of these individuals had any particular advantages. None of them had it easy. Their lives are evidence that there is no progress without struggle, no growth without uncertainty, no victory without the willingness to risk defeat. Something inside gave them strength, enabled them to press onward to their personal summit when most others would want to turn back. Their hearts were full of love for life and for their fellow man. They had faith in God and in the God-given abilities. They had hope that, with sacrifice and effort, they or anyone else can make a difference in this world, not necessarily by grand gesture or newsworthy feat, but by small acts, done patiently and with care.

The lives of these men and women, the example of their courage and faith, make us feel that we, too, are capable of something extraordinary, of leaving our "footprints on the sands of time." We recognize in those who realize their talents and abilities, who leave their indelible gift to the world, the part of ourselves that also can be great. We know, at the very core of our being, where truth and faith have not been marred by the falseness and cynicism of the world, that we can do something exceptional. It doesn't have to be on a grand scale, but where we are, with what we have, we can make the most of ourselves and give something of value to the world.

Perhaps our duty lies in educating ourselves, in further preparing for the tests and opportunities that lie ahead; perhaps there is a way, through our work and relations, to make this world a little safer, more honest and caring; perhaps there is someone who whose life we can touch ("He who saves a single person, it is as though he saved the whole world," remarked the Jewish sages). Discovering our purpose and then striving to fulfill it gives our lives meaning and satisfaction unknown to those who pursue a more shallow version of success.

The most acceptable service to God is doing good to man.

Benjamin Franklin

Few know their own strength.
It is in men as in soils, where sometimes there is a vein of gold which the owner knows not of.

Jonathan Swift

Lives of great men all remind us
We can make our lives sublime,
And, departing, leave behind us,
Footprints on the sands of time. . . .

Henry Wadsworth Longfellow

Few will have the greatness to bend history itself,
but each of us can work to change a small portion of events. . . .
It is from numberless acts of courage and belief
that human history is shaped.

Robert Kennedy

There is no road too long to one who advances deliberately
and without undue haste;
no honors too distant to one who prepares with patience.

Jean de La Bruyère

12
LIFE AFTER LOSS

Let nothing distress you, let nothing disturb you.
All things pass but God, who alone is sufficient.
St. Theresa of Avila

Sometimes, however, our calling is faint. Some of us are presently unable to move forward because life has dealt us a severe or tragic blow, and we are reeling in confusion and despair. Our energies are consumed and depressed; the "still small voice" that once urged us to do the greater thing is now scarcely audible, deadened by our pain.

Perhaps we are enduring a loss or a personal tragedy: the death of a loved one, a failed relationship, poor health, or the loss of a job, dream, or ideal. It is hard to think about living an extraordinary life, of reaching for the heights of our potential, of seizing the moment to partake of life's beauty and joy, when there is so much hurt inside. It is all we can do just to cope with the demands of daily living. We find ourselves on a frozen and desolate plain, struggling to keep moving or to set up camp so as not to succumb to the cold.

In the midst of such despair, we wonder if we will ever again feel warmth and see light. Forlornly, we recall the way things were before our present crisis—our passion, our sense of purpose, our ability to enjoy the sweetness and fullness of existence. Will these treasures ever be regained? Will we ever again be able to love and feel deeply, to overcome our numbness? Will we ever again have the faith and energy to do the things that we dream of? The answer is yes, we will, but with much patience and gentle effort. Also, hopefully, with the support of those willing to give us strength by sharing our pain—family, friends, clergy, competent professionals. There is a season for everything, and like all seasons, the season for healing must run its course. There is no measuring progress in days or weeks or even months, only by our ability to gradually regain what is best in ourselves.

Rabbi Pesach Krauss, former chaplain at Memorial Sloan-Kettering Cancer Center in New York, where he counseled patients and their families, tells an inspiring parable in his book *Why Me?* Two woodchoppers have cut down a tree that is well over a hundred years old. The younger man, observing the tree's growth rings, remarks that five of the rings are very close together. There must have been a five-year drought, he concludes, during which the tree experienced very little growth. The older timberman, however, known for his gentle wisdom, has a different perspective. The dry years were actually the most important years of the tree's life, he contends. Because of the drought, the tree had to force its roots deeper and deeper into the soil, in order to get the water and nourishment it needed. Then, when conditions improved, it was able to grow taller and faster because of its strengthened roots.

Likewise, our difficult times, the times when we are coping with loss or tragedy, can be times of great inner growth. Words cannot adequately describe the pain we may be enduring. Our emotional and spiritual suffering can be every bit as real and debilitating as physical suffering, and this is often difficult for others to recognize or understand. Yet with patient work, and faith in a better tomorrow, we will pass through our crisis, leaving one phase of our lives, but entering another which is bright and laden with potential. We will never be the same person we were before; our loss will always be with us. But with renewed strength and deepened sensitivity, we will be able to move on to new areas of growth, experience, fulfillment, and joy.

There is a budding morrow in midnight.
John Keats

The lowest ebb is the turn of the tide.
Henry Wadsworth Longfellow

The world breaks everyone,
and afterward many are strong in the broken places.

Ernest Hemingway

Although the world is full of suffering,
it is also full of the overcoming of it.

Helen Keller

Shared joy is double joy; shared sorrow is half sorrow.

Swedish Proverb

13
HEALING A BROKEN HEART

We are healed of a suffering only by experiencing it to the full.

Marcel Proust

For some the process of healing will be more lengthy and difficult than for others. Some people were injured early in life, as children. Someone perhaps neglected or hurt them, physically or emotionally, and all of their lives they have lacked courage and faith in themselves because their sense of value or worth was damaged at an early age. For them, the world is a dangerous place; they have learned that it is safer not to take risks, not to call attention to themselves. Or perhaps they are consumed with feelings of anger and resentment that hold them back from pursuing their dreams.

Jesus admonished anyone who would harm a child that it would be better that he tie a millstone around his neck and throw himself into the sea. Yet, tragically, many children are neglected and harmed, wittingly or unwittingly, by those who should cherish and protect them. This is the source of much of the world's suffering. It makes it difficult for many to open their hearts and to trust in all that is good in life. Furthermore, it is difficult or impossible for people to realize their talents and potentialities when their sense of value as human beings has been selfishly violated. "Self trust is the first secret of success," said Emerson. "Public opinion is a weak tyrant compared with our own private opinion," stated Thoreau. "The pious and just honoring of ourselves may be thought the fountainhead from whence every laudable and worthy enterprise issues forth," wrote Milton.

How can people in this situation, or any of us who have suffered a loss of self-worth, regain our birthright, our awareness of our wonderful gifts and potentialities? There are no easy answers, and for each of us the work that needs to be done will be necessarily different. Certainly, a first and important step is to seek the community of others who "bear the mark of pain." Their fellowship will be a source of strength and encouragement. We will realize that we are not alone in our suffering and that progress is indeed possible.

Beyond this, we must realize that spiritual and emotional healing, like physical healing, is gradual and best taken in small steps. Remember the truth of the proverb "A broken hand works, but not a broken heart." Go easy on yourself. Be patient as you would with a friend. Choose each day to do some small thing that affirms what you know to be true: that you are valuable and have an indomitable spirit that is capable of great love and happiness. Read a book that fills you with hope; listen to music that soothes your soul; take care of yourself by eating well, getting fresh air, exercise and rest ("Fatigue makes cowards of us all," said a wise soul). Make small decisions that silently claim your right to follow your higher aspirations and dreams. In time, these decisions will lead to greater ones, and you will draw courage and confidence from knowing that your life is directed towards wholeness and well-being. The important thing, it has been said, is not so much where we stand as in what direction our lives are moving.

Problems call forth our courage and our wisdom;
indeed, they create our courage and our wisdom.
It is only because of problems
that we grow mentally and spiritually.

M. Scott Peck

He who is outside his door
already has a hard part of his journey behind him.

Dutch Proverb

We need to get over the questions that focus on the past
and on the pain—"Why did this happen to me?"—
and ask instead the question which opens doors to the future:
"Now that this has happened, what shall I do about it?"

Rabbi Harold Kushner

When a man suffers, he ought not to say,
"That's bad! That's bad!" Nothing that God imposes on man is bad.
But it is all right to say,
"That's bitter!" For among medicines there are some
that are made with bitter herbs.

Hasidic Saying

I do not believe that sheer suffering teaches.
If suffering alone taught, all the world would be wise,
since everyone suffers. To suffering must be added mourning,
understanding, patience, love, openness
and the willingness to remain vulnerable.

Anne Morrow Lindbergh

14
A "PEACE WHICH PASSETH ALL UNDERSTANDING"

Would that life were like the shadow cast by a wall or a tree, but it is like the shadow of a bird in flight.
The Talmud

A number of years ago, in Europe, there was a terrible accident, and forty men were trapped in a coal mine, where they suffocated to death. Their devastated families gathered at the entrance to the mine, and the spiritual leader of the community came to address the crowd. He hoped to offer words of comfort and guidance. According to Sidney Greenberg, in his beautiful book *A Treasury of Comfort,* this is what he said:

"What happened here is a mystery, impossible for us to understand. But I want to tell you about something I have at home. It's a bookmark that my mother embroidered and gave to me many years ago. On one side, the threads go this way and that, crisscrossed in wild and colorful confusion, and when you look at it, you would wonder if she had any idea what she was doing. But then, when you turn it over, on the other side you see the words 'God is love,' beautifully spelled out in silken threads. Now, today we are looking at this tragedy from one side, and it makes no sense. But someday we will be permitted to glimpse its meaning from the other side. Meanwhile, let us wait and trust."

When we are in the midst of suffering, it is difficult to see clearly. It is as though we were looking at the back of the bookmark, where all the embroidery threads are tangled and confused. In my own spiritual walk, I have found that turning to God during such difficult times can be a source of great comfort and guidance. In the Gospel of Matthew, there is a story about Peter, who in the midst of a storm gets out of a boat and tries to walk across the water to Jesus. As long as he keeps his eyes focused on Jesus, he does fine. But as soon as he starts thinking about the howling winds and rough seas, he becomes frightened and starts to sink. Likewise, I've found that if I reach out to God in the midst of my trials, I will regain my sense of balance and wholeness; I will begin to experience what Paul called a "peace which passeth all understanding." But if I do not turn to God and focus only on my problem or my loss, then I can become fearful and feel that I am sinking.

Shakespeare wrote in *Hamlet* that there is more to life than is dreamt of in our systems of philosophy. I believe that this is true and that the miracle of our existence should give us every confidence that there can be miracle beyond it—it is not a big step to go from accepting one to having faith in the other. If we open ourselves up to this miracle beyond a miracle, it will often lead us to a place of acceptance and peace.

Sometimes turning to God can be difficult, especially when we are numb and reeling in the pain, especially when our hearts have been deeply wounded. But here is another story that might help. This story is from the Talmud, which is a collection of holy books written centuries ago by Jewish sages and scholars. The story is about a rabbi who went to the synagogue on the Sabbath to pray for the whole day. While he was gone, something terrible happened, and his twin infant sons died unexpectedly in their sleep.

The rabbi's wife knew that her husband was going to be devastated by the loss of their sons, whom they both loved very much. When he returned from the synagogue, she met him at the door. First she asked him to recite a prayer with her, and then she said, "My husband, I have a question for you. Not long ago, some precious jewels were entrusted to my care. Do you remember? Their beauty has brought much joy to my life. Now their owner has returned and wants the jewels back. What should I do? Should I return them?"

"Of course, you should return them," said the rabbi. "You know the Law. Naturally you must return what is not yours."

At that time, the wife took her husband by the hand and led him to his two sons.

"Oh, my sons! My sons!" the rabbi lamented, realizing what had happened.

And then his wife reminded him, with tears in her eyes, "But did you not say that we must give back to the owner what has been entrusted to our care? Our sons were like precious jewels that God entrusted to us. Now He has taken them back as His own." And the husband and wife fell into each other's arms and wept.

God is closest to those with broken hearts.

Jewish Proverb

People bring us well-meant but miserable consolations
when they tell us what time will do to help our grief.
We do not want to lose our grief,
because our grief is bound up with our love and we could not cease
to mourn without being robbed of our affections.

Phillips Brooks

Nothing can fill the gap when we are away from those we love,
and it would be wrong to try to find anything. . . .
God does not fill it, but keeps it empty so that our communion
with another may be kept alive, even at the cost of pain.

Dietrich Bonhoeffer

All I have seen teaches me to trust the Creator for all I have not seen.

Ralph Waldo Emerson

As we pray continually,
even during times when God seems distant
and prayer feels fruitless, we immerse ourselves in the benevolence,
forgiveness, and love of God.

Jimmy Carter

15
LETTING GO

You cannot prevent the birds of sadness from passing over your head, but you can prevent them from nesting in your hair.

Swedish Proverb

Sometimes, when it comes to suffering over a failed relationship or a shattered dream, we can make the situation worse for ourselves by holding on too long, by not letting go. We get ourselves into a rut, which, someone has observed, can be like a grave without ends.

How can we avoid doing this? Perhaps another story will be helpful, this one a folktale from France adapted here from a collection by Henri Pourrat. According to this tale, a certain man set out his traps to catch some birds. When he returned the next day, he had caught a single nightingale, which he took out of the cage and held in his hand.

Before he could kill the tiny bird with his thumb, the nightingale surprised him by speaking. "Stop, please," said the bird, "you have nothing to gain by killing me. You can see that I'm too small to satisfy your hunger. But I have a proposal: let me go, and I will give you three pieces of advice that you will find of great value, if you will only put them to use."

The man replied, "If your advice is as good as you say, I'll let you go."

"All right, then, listen carefully," said the nightingale. "First, don't go after something that is beyond your reach. Second, don't agonize over what is hopelessly lost. Third, don't stubbornly believe in something that defies belief."

As he pondered the nightingale's advice, the man momentarily relaxed his grip. At once, the nightingale flew out of his hand and perched on the branch of a nearby tree.

"You foolish man!" said the bird. "You set me free, and all the while I had a treasure in my breast—a golden nugget the size of a plum!"

The man's jaw dropped. Such a large piece of gold, and he had had it in his grasp! He was almost sick with dismay, and he looked for a stone to throw at the bird. But then he realized that the nightingale would fly out of range if he threatened it, and he would never see it again. So instead he tried to coax it down from the tree.

"Come here, little bird," he said, his throat tight with anger. "Come with me and I will take you to my house and give you a place of honor. Everything you can possibly want will be yours."

"You poor man," said the nightingale from atop the tree. "You're even more foolish than I had thought. Look at what you have done with my three bits of advice; you've let them rush through your head as the wind rushes through the trees!

"As you can see, I'm beyond your reach, yet you insist on going after me. I'm hopelessly lost to you, and yet you are sick with grief and can't let go. Finally, how is it possible that I have a golden nugget inside my breast? Does that not defy belief? Yet you insist on believing it. My poor man!"

With that, the nightingale flew away, and the man was left to think about the wise advice that he had failed to follow.

Another folktale, this one Chinese and found in many collections, reveals how we sometimes assume that a particular loss or setback is bad for us, when the reverse might actually be the case. This can be especially true when it comes to a lost opportunity, a dream delayed, or a relationship that has not fulfilled our expectations.

According to this tale, there once lived a wise man who made his home in the foothills of a range of great snow-capped mountains. The man owned many horses, and one day one of his mares ran off. His family and friends helped him search for the mare, but they couldn't find it. They comforted the man and said that they were sorry for his misfortune, but he replied, "What makes you so sure that this is not a blessing?"

Several days later, the wise man looked in the direction of the mountains and saw two horses trotting toward his house. One was his lost mare, and a splendid wild stallion followed her. The man's family and friends congratulated him for his good fortune, for the stallion was certainly of great worth. But the man replied, "What makes you so sure this is not a disaster?"

Some time later, the man's son, who had been trying to train the stallion, took it out for a ride. The horse became agitated and threw him. He fell to the ground and broke his leg. Family and friends tried to console the old man, but he said, "What makes you so sure this is not a blessing?"

About a month later, the province became engaged in a cruel war against nomad invaders. All able-bodied young men were enlisted, and nine out of ten lost their lives. Because the old man's son was laid up with a badly broken leg, he was unable to go to war, and he survived. He took care of his aging father for many years after that, giving him beautiful grandchildren and moments of great joy.

The old man's family and friends were amazed at how a blessing can turn into a disaster, and a disaster into a blessing, and how no one can truly know what is to come.

Life is an onion which we peel crying.

French Proverb

It is one of life's laws that as soon as one door closes,
another one opens.
But the tragedy is that we look at the closed door
and disregard the open one.

André Gide

He is wise who does not grieve for the things which he has not,
but rejoices for those which he has.

Epictetus

We often find that our prayers bring about change,
at least in ourselves, as God opens our eyes to a better future.

Jimmy Carter

The Lord is near to all who call on him.

Psalms 145:18

16
HOW TO AVOID A LIFE OF QUIET DESPERATION

To know what you prefer, instead of saying "Amen" to what the world tells you that you ought to prefer, is to keep your soul alive.

Robert Louis Stevenson

For some, the task of the moment is to heal, to regain our sense of value, to patiently turn our lives back in the right direction. Many of us, however, are not passing through the darkness of a personal crisis or tragedy. We have survived our loss, we have grown through our pain. We have reasonable confidence in ourselves and in our ability to affect the world in which we live. But still we do not act. Though able to hear the "still small voice" that urges us to reach for our dream, or to grow and blossom where we are, we do not answer the call. We do not take the requisite step of faith and make our necessary parting with the crowd.

Instead, we do what is common, yielding to our natural inclination for ease and pleasure (goals that Albert Einstein commented are "more proper for a herd of swine"), or we do what others say we should do, displacing what we value by giving importance to what others seem to value: financial and material prosperity, power and position. One finds it "too venturesome a thing to be himself," observed Søren Kierkegaard, "far easier to be an imitation, a number, a cipher in the crowd." As a result, we live in a prison of our own making. We set our own limits and wittingly hold ourselves back from the richer and fuller life, from the greater sense of adventure and satisfaction, that is possible for us. And, tragically, we deprive the world, those with whom our invaluable, brief existence comes into contact, of our most sincere gift. In a sense, a part of us dies before our death.

In his short novel *The Death of Ivan Ilyich,* Leo Tolstoy tells the story of a man whose chief ambitions in life have been wealth, power, and the esteem of the upper class. In pursuit of these, he sacrifices his own dreams and ideals, and adopts the values of those whom he so much admires. In effect, he becomes a stranger to himself, losing touch with important facets of his personality, replacing the true with the false. "All of the passion of youth and childhood had passed away," writes Tolstoy, "not leaving serious traces."

On Ivan's deathbed, it occurs to him that, even though he has been successful in terms of wealth and position, even though he has bought the right furniture and invited the right people to his house for dinner, maybe his life has really been a failure. "Maybe I did not live as I ought to have done," Ivan thinks, "But how can that be, when I did everything properly?"

Tolstoy writes that Ivan dismisses from his mind the troubling question of whether he lived a good life. But the terrible thought keeps coming back. Perhaps he did not live in the right way; perhaps success is something different than he had thought. "It was as if I had been going downhill while I imagined I was going up," Ivan realizes. "And that is really what it was. I was going up in public opinion, but to the same extent life was ebbing away from me. And now it is all done and there is only death."

Could it be that many of us are going downhill when we think we are going up? Could the passion and ideals, the talents and dreams, the raw sensitivity of our youth, be slipping away from us as we adopt the values and goals of those around us? What makes Ivan's situation tragic, and his death agonizing, is that he does not realize the falseness of his life until it is practically too late. But we may be more fortunate. There may still be time to turn from mediocrity and conformity, from laziness and fear, and to follow the path with heart. We may yet have the chance to express greater love and originality in the place where we stand, or, if we are so inclined, to take small steps—if not a giant leap—toward our most cherished dreams and aspirations.

Let us endeavor so to live that when we come to die,
even the undertaker will be sorry.

Mark Twain

The measure of a person's life is the well spending of it,
and not the length.

Plutarch

To act without clear understanding, to form habits without investigation, to follow a path all one's life without knowing where it really leads, such is the behavior of the multitude.

Mencius

The great thing is to be at one's post as a child of God, living each day as though it were our last, but planning as though our world might last a hundred years.

C. S. Lewis

What I must do is all that concerns me,
not what the people think. . . .
You will always find those who think they know what is your duty
better than you know it. It is easy in the world to live after the
world's opinion; it is easy in solitude to live after our own;
but the great man is he who in the midst of the crowd
keeps with perfect sweetness the independence of solitude.

Ralph Waldo Emerson

17
YOUR MOST PRECIOUS POSSESSION—AND HOW TO PROTECT IT

Our heart changes, and this is the greatest cause of suffering in life.

Marcel Proust

In our youth, we are passionate for all that is good in the world, sensitive to all that could be better. Our emotions are raw and tingle on the surface of our being. A beautiful song can bring us to tears, a statement of truth can pierce our hearts; suffering elicits our deepest sympathy, injustice our most scalding enmity and indignation. We feel ourselves to be in touch with God and with our fellow human beings. We are participants in the world and our lives stretch out before us, lined with possibilities.

As we grow older, however, the ideals and convictions that are precious to us in youth may be steadily dissolved by the hardships and exigencies of life. A man "once believed in the victory of truth," observed Schweitzer, "now he no longer does. He believed in humanity; that is over. He believed in the Good; that is over. He eagerly sought justice; that is over. He trusted in the power of kindness and peaceableness; that is over. He could become enthusiastic; that is over. In order to steer more safely through the perils and storms of life, he has lightened his boat. He has thrown overboard goods that he considered dispensable. But the ballast he dumped was actually his food and drink. Now he skims more lightly over the waves, but he is hungry and parched."

Holding on to our ideals and convictions is perhaps the most difficult thing any of us has to do. Inevitably, we all run up against hardships and obstacles that tempt us to abandon what we know to be right and to take an easier path. A young woman who wants to be a doctor decides that the years of hard work and rigorous training are too much to bear, and she takes an easier job that for her has little meaning and does not make use of her special gifts. A young man gives up on his dream to compose or perform music, to partake in one of humanity's most beautiful achievements, because his family or friends staunchly remind him of the pitfalls and dangers of an artist's career. Still another person, perhaps a bit older, decides to compromise his sense of values—values that once gave his life meaning—in order to make a quick profit or to enjoy some fleeting pleasure or illicit return. "It's what everyone else does," he rationalizes. "I'm only human. Nobody's perfect."

It is a sorry day when we give up what is best in ourselves, when we sacrifice the values and ideals that give our lives meaning, for some temporary advantage. In doing so we lose something more precious than anything we could possibly gain, and we create an emptiness in the pit of our being that becomes difficult to fill. "In youthful idealism man perceives the truth," wrote Schweitzer. "In youthful idealism he possesses riches that should not be bartered for anything on earth."

There is an old Jewish tale about a rabbi who discusses being true to one's ideals and the temptations of life with three of his disciples. At one point he asks them, "What would you do if you found a large sum of money?"

The first disciple responds, "I'd return it to its owner."

"I don't believe you," says the rabbi. "You are much too quick with your answer."

The second disciple answers, "If no one saw me, I'd keep the money for myself."

"You are open and frank, but you cannot be trusted!" says the rabbi.

Finally, the third disciple ventures an answer. "I would be very tempted to keep the money," he says, "But I would pray to God that he save me from evil and give me the strength to do what is right."

The rabbi smiles and says, "May God bless you! You are a person I can trust!"

The great person is he who does not lose his child's heart.

Chinese Proverb

Always do right. This will gratify some people and astonish the rest.

Mark Twain

The young do not know enough to be prudent,
and therefore they attempt the impossible—and achieve it,
generation after generation.

Pearl S. Buck

Far away in the sunshine are my highest aspirations.
I may not reach them, but I can look up and see their beauty,
believe in them and try to follow where they lead.

Louisa May Alcott

The youth gets together his materials to build a bridge to the moon,
or perchance a palace or temple on the earth,
and at length the middle-aged man concludes
to build a woodshed with them.

Henry David Thoreau

18
TO THINE OWN SELF BE TRUE

If you build according to everyone's advice,
you will have a crooked house.
Danish Proverb

As we grow up, there is the constant pressure to conform, to fit in. From our earliest years, we want to be liked, we want to be part of the group. This is human; we need each other deeply. What is more, being an outcast is painful, and others can be shockingly cruel and adept at administering the pain. Consequently, we sometimes make the mistake of smoothing out the edges of our personality in order to be accepted. We chip and sand away at our truest values, at our most cherished ideals, and then add others that fit poorly in their place, because we are justifiably afraid of standing alone.

Tragically, however, if others accept or admire the person we have created, we still are not at ease. They accept an image we present, not us; they admire a counterfeit person, an imposter, not the person we know in our hearts we are or can be. Thus our conformity is self-defeating. Even in success we feel like a failure. Even with others we feel alone. True community, true love and acceptance, can only be born of truth.

Moreover, in conforming and trying to fit in, we should know that we will never be able to please everyone. There is a classic tale, told for centuries in Africa, Asia, and Europe and adapted here from a retelling by James Baldwin, that illustrates this principle. It's about a man, a boy, and a donkey who are on their way to market when someone on the road remarks, "Why are you leading that donkey behind you? What good is a donkey if you do not ride upon it?"

"Thanks for the advice," says the man. "I am happy to please you." And he puts the boy on the donkey's back.

Soon they pass a group of old men, and one of them says, "How shameful. That lazy boy rides the donkey and makes his poor father walk."

When the man hears this, his asks the boy to get off and mounts the donkey himself. "Let's see if we can't please these men," he says.

They travel a bit farther and meet two women on the road. The women say to each other, loud enough so the man can hear, "Look at that lazy man. He takes it easy and makes his poor boy walk behind."

Now the man is getting confused. "My son, how are we going to please everybody?" Pondering the situation, he reaches down and pulls his son up on the donkey with him. And they continue their journey.

Entering the village, they notice a crowd of people pointing and jeering at them. "What's the matter?" says the man.

"You ought to be ashamed of yourselves for being so cruel to that poor old donkey," they say. "You are much too heavy for such an animal."

"I hadn't thought of that," says the man. "You are probably right, but we were only trying to please some friends."

So the man and the boy get off the donkey and think over their situation. Finally, the man gets an idea. He and his son find a long pole, and they tie the donkey's feet to it. Then, with much grunting and groaning, they lift the pole on their shoulders and begin to walk again carrying the donkey. The donkey looks displeased, but there is nothing it can do about it.

The man and the boy struggle under the load, and the people of the village laugh at the unusual sight. "I think we are pleasing everybody now," says the man to his son.

Finally, while they are crossing a bridge to the marketplace, the donkey's hooves start to slip through the ropes. The animal kicks and brays, and this makes the man and the boy stumble and drop the pole. The donkey falls over the edge of the bridge into the river and drowns.

Sitting in the middle of the bridge, the man says to his son, "I think there is a lesson to be learned from all of this."

"What is the lesson, Father?"

"If you try to please everyone, you will end up pleasing no one."

This above all: to thine own self be true, And it must follow, as the night the day, Thou canst not be false to any man.

William Shakespeare

It is better to fail in originality than to succeed in imitation.

Herman Melville

Insist on yourself; never imitate.

Ralph Waldo Emerson

A wildflower on the mountaintop
would not change places with a rose in the garden.

Armenian Proverb

The greatest thing in the world is to know how to be one's own self.

Michel de Montaigne

19
MARCH TO A DIFFERENT DRUMMER

Why should we be in such desperate haste to succeed
and in such desperate enterprises?
If a man does not keep pace with his companions,
perhaps it is because he hears a different drummer.
Let him step to the music he hears, however measured or far away.

Henry David Thoreau

Some writers and philosophers have looked upon conformity and the desire to please as emasculating influences that stunt the growth and inhibit the power of the world's most noble and stalwart spirits. For example, in one startling aphorism, the philosopher Friedrich Nietzsche claimed that all truly great lives have been like glaciers that have cut their way across mountains, reducing to rubble everything that stands in their way, first being agents of destruction. But some time later, grass, wildflowers, and trees spring from the ground, and the treacherous paths cut by the glaciers become beautiful, verdant valleys, nourished by rich soil and flowing streams, bursting with life.

Like a glacier, Nietzsche calls on his readers to be willing to destroy the norms of the culture in which they live, to break away from the "herd" and to live by their own standards, even if considered evil. The metaphor is striking, and perhaps there is truth in it. The artist Picasso remarked, "Every act of creation is first of all an act of destruction." And Rollo May writes, "Whenever there is a breakthrough of a significant idea in science or a significant new form in art, the new idea will destroy what a lot of people believe is essential to the survival of their intellectual and spiritual world."

Although there is truth in these insights, even the freshest water when blended with poison can be lethal. The obvious danger is that if our foremost concern is not for the well- being of other people and the world in which we live—if we are motivated by the desire to destroy rather than to build, by power and selfishness rather than by love and what Schweitzer called *reverence for life*—then almost any action can be justified, even the heinous acts of a Hitler or Stalin. There would be little chance of our survival; indeed, the world in which we might survive would be a dark and terrifying place.

Our independence must therefore be tempered, paradoxically, by dependence; our need to stand alone by our need to stand together; our desire to break away by our desire to mend and make whole. "If I am not for myself, who will be for me? *And being for my own self, what am I?*" Rabbi Hillel asks in the Talmud (emphasis added). "We are called to be individuals. We are called to be unique and different . . ." writes M. Scott Peck in *The Different Drum*, "yet the reality is that we are inevitably social creatures who desperately need each other not merely for sustenance, not merely for company, but for any meaning to our lives whatsoever."

Once a father gathered his sons and handed each of them a stick. "Try to break the stick," he said to them, and they each did so easily.

"Now," said the father, "which of you would like to try his hand at breaking this bundle of sticks."

The strongest son volunteered and the father handed him the bundle of sticks. The young man tried as hard as he could, but he could not break them.

"Let this be a lesson to you," said the father. "United, you are strong. Apart, you are vulnerable and weak."

We must learn to live together as brothers or perish together as fools.

Martin Luther King, Jr.

Two are better than one; . . .
for if they fall, the one will lift up his fellow.

Ecclesiastes 4:9–10

We cannot live only for ourselves.
A thousand fibers connect us with our fellow men;
and along these fibers, as sympathetic threads,
our actions run as causes, and they come back to us as effects.

Herman Melville

"These things I command you, that ye love one another."

Jesus in John 15:17

A joyful heart is the inevitable result of a heart burning with love.

Mother Teresa

20
BALANCING COURAGE WITH CAUTION

That is a wise delay that makes the road safe.
Spanish Proverb

Even if you have a dream that could benefit others, even if you have a vision of a better world and are willing to endure the pain that inevitably accompanies growth and the insecurity that inevitably accompanies going forth into the unknown, the people in your life may feel uncomfortable and try to persuade you to remain where you are. They may ridicule you or be all too willing to remind you of your limits and the dangers of the path you wish to follow.

For example, Albert Schweitzer's family tried to call his attention to the "folly" of his desire to serve as a doctor in Africa. Anton Dvořák's father tried to persuade his son to become a butcher rather than a composer. Handel's father reportedly wanted him to be a lawyer; Cézanne's, a businessman. Isaac Newton's mother wanted him to run the family farm and did not like his reading so many books. Florence Nightingale's family thought it better that she get married and live a quiet and comfortable life rather than enter the profession of nursing, which at the time was considered disreputable.

Why is this? Why do those around us, sometimes those

closest in our lives, often try to hold us back from fulfilling our highest potential? Perhaps in part because in pursuing our dreams, we remind them, consciously or unconsciously, of their forsaken ideals, of their undeveloped talents; maybe they want everyone and everything around them, insofar as possible, to validate their own choices, their own path in life. Or perhaps they are genuinely concerned that we may suffer or fail, not realizing that the pursuit of our dreams and the progressive realization of our talents, even though they may not make us a lot of money or always produce the results we desire, is success, and that fear, following the wrong path or trying to stay where we are, no matter how comfortable and secure we may be, is failure.

Or perhaps those who love us are afraid of change. Life can be confusing and maybe they want their world, and the people in it, somehow to stand still and to be understandable, to fit neatly into their conception of things. What they do not realize is that to develop our talents, to make use of our greatest abilities, it is necessary to change, it is necessary to move step by step from the plains of mediocrity and farther up the path with heart, to the glorious peaks where we have a clearer view of life and of ourselves. The philosopher Henri Bergson wrote, "To change is to mature, and to mature is to go on creating oneself endlessly."

Sometimes, however, those who love us may have good reason to be concerned about our safety and well-being, and we would be wise to listen to them, as is demonstrated in the classic myth of Icarus and Daedalus. As you might recall, Daedalus and his son were imprisoned in a tower by the sea in Crete. Even if they could escape the tower, getting away by sea was impossible, because ships were being searched for stowaways. So Daedalus, who was the greatest inventor of his time, spent weeks collecting feathers of all sizes. He molded these feathers with wax into two pairs of great wings, shaped like those of seagulls. Then, when the wind was just right, he and his son strapped on the wings, jumped from the tower, and took flight.

"Remember," Daedalus told Icarus, "do not fly too low or the ocean spray will weigh down your wings. Do not fly too high or the sun will melt the wax, and they will fall apart."

At first they flew with trepidation. The rocky coast and the crashing waves beneath them seemed ominous; falling would mean certain death. But with time they gained confidence, and they began to enjoy the freedom of flight.

A farmer on the ground looked up and his jaw dropped in disbelief. Children, playing in the fields, saw them and waved. Quickly, word spread, and people ran out of their houses to witness the two figures in the sky. Could they be gods?

Icarus looked down at the people, the land, and the ships on the sea. He was filled with excitement and soared higher and higher, forgetting his father's warning.

"Icarus, come back!" Daedalus cried. "Your wings will melt! You're getting too close to the sun!"

But Icarus flew higher, consumed by the glory and excitement of the moment. As he got nearer to the sun, the wax on his wings started to get soft. Feathers began to scatter in the air, and then, suddenly, his wings came apart. Icarus moved his arms and tried to keep himself in the air, but there was nothing he could do. He cried out to his father, who was looking on with horror, and he fell thousands of feet to his death in the sea.

The tale is tragic and it reminds us that our safety requires a measure of obedience, especially to our parents when we are not yet adults. It's easy to forget, but our parents often know better. Though they might seem out of step with the times, they probably have a great deal more wisdom and experience than we would like to admit.

However, not all of us who pursue our dreams are so rash as to fly too close to the sun. As we mature, we know that we must balance courage with caution, perseverance with prudence. At the same time, we know that if everyone were motivated by fear, then nothing innovative or revolutionary would ever take place, nothing creative or progressive would ever be achieved. Therefore, we try to respect and keep alive our aspirations and dreams.

When I was a boy of fourteen, my father was so ignorant I could hardly stand to have the old man around.
But when I got to be twenty-one,
I was astonished at how much he had learned in seven years.

Mark Twain

Ask the young; they know everything.

French Proverb

Have you learned lessons only from those who admire you, and were tender with you, and stood aside for you? Have you not learned great lessons from those who rejected you, and braced themselves against you, or disputed the passage with you?

Walt Whitman

If it is possible, as far as it depends on you,
at peace with everyone. . . .
Do not be overcome by evil, but overcome evil with good.

Romans 12:17–21

Good for good is only fair;
Bad for bad soon brings despair;
Bad for good is vile and base;
Good for bad shows forth God's grace.

Welsh Folk Saying

21
HOW TO CONQUER RESISTANCE WITH LOVE AND TRUTH

No person resolved to make the most of himself can spare time for personal contention.

Abraham Lincoln

Since "everything new meets resistance," to quote a proverb, how can we stand up to those who may oppose us? How can we win over those who might fear for our safety or want us to conform to their ideals, rather than our own? How can we protect the ties of love and the bonds of sympathy that are so vital to our individual and collective well-being?

The answer lies in the tradition of civil disobedience practiced by Socrates, Jesus, Mahatma Gandhi, and Martin Luther King, Jr. If others stand in our way, it is counterproductive to meet them with violence, whether this violence be physical or emotional—we may gain the world and lose our soul—and neither should we give in or acquiesce to what we know is wrong. Rather, we must resist with all the force of our being, opposing them with love and understanding, with a willingness to suffer and endure rather than resort to violence or submit to their will.

"The old law of an eye for an eye leaves everyone blind," wrote Martin Luther King, Jr. "It is immoral because it seeks to humiliate the opponent rather than win his understanding; it seeks to annihilate rather than to convert. Violence is immoral because it thrives on hatred rather than love. It destroys community and makes brotherhood impossible. It leaves society in a monologue rather than a dialogue. Violence ends by defeating itself. It creates bitterness in survivors and brutality in destroyers." And in another passage King states, "The non-violent approach does not immediately change the heart of the oppressor. It first does something to the hearts and souls of those committed to it. It gives them new self-respect; it calls up resources of strength and courage that they did not know they had. Finally, it reaches the opponent and so stirs his conscience that reconciliation becomes a reality."

If our path is blocked, we must resist those who block it with patience, love, and understanding. Perhaps they have good reason, and we can learn from them. However, if the path we wish to follow is right, and if we resist the forces that oppose us in the spirit of friendship and civility but resist them nonetheless with all of the strength of our being, with what Gandhi called *satyagraha,* meaning the force of love and truth, then others will come to see the validity of our vision, and, in admiration for our determination, in compassion for our willingness to suffer for what we know is right, they might even become allies and support us in our cause.

It has been said that one of Abraham Lincoln's advisers commented, "Mr. President, I cannot understand you. You treat your enemies with such kindness. It would seem to me that you should want to destroy them." Lincoln replied, "My dear fellow, I do destroy my enemy when I make him into a friend."

Love is the only force capable of transforming
an enemy into a friend.
Hate destroys and tears down. . . .
Love creates and builds up.
Martin Luther King, Jr.

If you would win a man to your cause,
first convince him that you are his sincere friend.
Therein is a drop of honey that catches his heart.
Abraham Lincoln

He is wise who can make a friend of a foe.
Scottish Proverb

To those who are good to me, let me be good.
To those who are not good to me, let me also be good.
Thus shall goodness be increased.

Lao Tzu

Lord, make me an instrument of your peace:
Where there is hatred, let me sow love;
Where there is injury, pardon;
Where there is doubt, faith;
Where there is despair, hope;
Where there is darkness, light;
And where there is sadness, joy.
O Divine Master, grant that I may not so
much seek to be consoled, as to console,
to be understood, as to understand,
to be loved, as to love;
for it is in giving that we receive,
it is in pardoning that we are pardoned, and
it is in dying that we are born to eternal life.

St. Francis of Assisi

22
YOU CAN BE A PERSON OF ACTION

One can choose to go back toward safety or forward toward growth.
Growth must be chosen again and again;
fear must be overcome again and again.
Abraham Maslow

Discovering precisely what we wish to do in life is no easy task. It requires continued discipline and resolve for a person, young or old, to mute the constant noise and banter of the world in which we live, to be alone and in perfect stillness with the dictates of his or her soul. But this is precisely what is necessary if we are to hear our higher cal-ling and follow our path with heart. Our modern world is so busy, so restless and full of activity, that it has become increasingly difficult for us to find the peace and tranquillity that are necessary to be in touch with the higher part of our own nature and to contemplate the course of our short and unrepeatable lives.

The French historian Alexis de Tocqueville, after traveling in the United States over 150 years ago, wrote that he had never seen a less philosophical society, noting, "Their life is so practical, so confused, so excited, so active, that little time remains for them for thought." The situation is, if anything, worse today. Not only are we in a terrible rush to succeed, to reach a certain level of material and financial prosperity that we believe will lead to our well-being and happiness, but we are also barraged from all sides with every manner of information, some of which is useful and entertaining but much of which is wholly irrelevant to our growth and fulfillment in life. We are surrounded with the constant stimulus of television, radio, computers, newspapers, and magazines. Countless advertisements, written, spoken, and visual, appeal to our baser impulses and urge us to buy all kinds of products and services, to follow the latest trends, and to dress, act, and look a certain way so that we may keep up with those around us. Our mental diet is, to a large degree, void of nutrients; we subsist on the intellectual equivalent of fats and sugars and suffer from the stunted growth, anxiety, depression, and mental lethargy that inevitably result from such imbalance.

It is difficult, and it requires continued discipline and determination, to maintain our sense of direction and integrity in a world that in so many ways, blatant and subtle, conspires against us. It is far easier to give up and stop caring. In *The Snows of Kilimanjaro,* Ernest Hemingway tells the story of a man who sacrifices his talents as a writer to his all-too-human desire for comfort and ease. On a safari with his wealthy wife, he has contracted gangrene and lies dying on a hot and dusty African plain, just below beautiful ice-capped Mt. Kilimanjaro.

The disease has progressed so far that the nerves in his infected leg have been killed; although there is no pain, there is a terrible smell, and hideous vultures have begun circling and landing nearby, waiting. The man knows that death is imminent.

Lying on his cot, the man thinks back on all the stories he had planned to write, that it had been his duty to write, but that he never completed. Instead he had saved them until he knew enough to write them well. His considerable talents had helped him enter the society of the very rich (where he met his present wife, his "caretaker"), and for the past several years he has languished in pleasure and comfort, no longer making use of his gifts as a writer. This slowly drained his passion and desire. "Each day of not writing, of comfort," writes Hemingway, "of being that which he despised, dulled his ability and softened his will to work so that, finally, he did no work at all. Now he would not have another chance." The man's death is physically painless, but like that of Ivan Ilyich in Tolstoy's story, it is spiritually agonizing for him as he looks back on his squandered talents and ideals, on his wasted life.

All of us who wish to do something with our lives must come to terms with our natural inclination for ease and comfort, with our natural reluctance to make a commitment and take action. "There are risks and costs to a program of action, but they are far less than the long-range risks and costs of comfortable inaction," said John F. Kennedy in a statement that is as valid spiritually and psychologically as it is politically. Staying where we are, waiting for just the right moment to act on our dreams, can give us a false feeling of power and potential. Rather than truly making the most of our talents at work, rather than pursuing our ideal, we can tell ourselves that we will do so, perhaps tomorrow or next week. We can harbor the comforting illusion that we can do something special without the pain and risks that would accompany decision and action.

There a price for this inaction; for at a deeper level, at the core of our being, which somehow knows the truth, we sense that we are deceiving ourselves and that, to be whole, we must have courage and take action. With each passing day, however, our resolve weakens, and we become progressively incapable of initiative and work. "Iron rusts from disuse," wrote Leonardo da Vinci in his journals; "water loses its purity from stagnation and in cold weather becomes frozen; even so does inaction sap the vigor of the mind." And the French essayist Michel de Montaigne observed, "The most outstanding gifts can be destroyed by idleness."

Laziness may appear attractive, but work gives satisfaction.

Anne Frank

*There is always hope in a man that actually and earnestly works;
in idleness alone is there perpetual despair.*

Thomas Carlyle

*Shun idleness.
It is a rust that attaches itself to the most brilliant metals.*

Voltaire

*Knowing is not enough, we must apply;
willing is not enough, we must do.*

Goethe

*Far better it is to dare mighty things,
to win glorious triumphs even though checkered by failure,
than to take rank with those poor spirits
who neither enjoy nor suffer much,
because they live in the gray twilight
that knows not victory nor defeat.*

Theodore Roosevelt

23
LIVING A BALANCED LIFE

Take a rest. The field that has rested gives a beautiful crop.

Ovid

Life is difficult, and we all need periods of rest to help restore our energy and enthusiasm. What is more, it seems wrong to get so caught up in our work, in our desire to grow and to fulfill our potential, that we lose our ability to enjoy the natural treasures of life. Seizing the moment to enjoy life is a talent in itself that we must also develop and express. Like other talents, it will slowly atrophy and disappear if we do not nurture it and make it grow. "The great man is he who does not lose his child's heart," said the Chinese philosopher Mencius. "There is more to life than increasing its speed," cautioned Gandhi. "In the world to come, each of us will be called to account for all the good things God put on earth that we refused to enjoy," it says in the Talmud.

Therefore, as in many areas of life, it is wise to seek moderation, to strike a balance between rest and work, comfort and worthwhile pursuits. In a similar manner, if we are so inclined, it is wise to seek a balance between prayer and action, contemplation and service. According to the Gospel of Luke, a woman named Martha once opened her home to Jesus as he traveled through Bethany in Palestine. Her sister, Mary, sat at Jesus' feet listening to all he had to say, while Martha was distracted by the preparations she had to make in order to be a gracious hostess. Martha said to Jesus, "Lord, do you not care that my sister has left me to do all the work by myself? Tell her to help me!"

"Martha, Martha," Jesus replied. "You are anxious and bothered by many things, but only one thing is needed. Mary has chosen the better part, and it will not be taken away from her." What was the better part that Mary had chosen? It was sitting at Jesus' feet and listening to him with love.

Many of us today can relate to Martha. We, too, are anxious and bothered by many things; we, too, are busy doing our work, paying our bills, trying to be good parents, friends, and neighbors. Though these works are important (in fact, in the Gospel of Luke, the Parable of the Good Samaritan comes just before the story of Mary and Martha), Jesus reminds his listeners that they are not the "better part." The better part, we can surmise, lies in a deeper personal union with God.

Throughout his ministry, Jesus set an example of balancing action with prayer, works with faith. He prayed, for example, in the desert, on the mountain, in the Temple, at the table, in the garden, and on the cross. He said, in the Gospel of John, "I can do nothing by myself. My aim is to do not my own will, but the will of Him who sent me." And, "It is the Father living in me who is doing this work."

In turning to God in prayer, which can mean simply talking and listening to Him or writing to Him in a journal, we can find our world being transformed from confusion to order, anxiety to serenity, and despair to hope. We can be inspired with new goals and creative ways to meet difficult challenges. In a sense, God becomes our teacher and guide. As Jimmy Carter has written, "Living in harmony with the omnipotent God makes us stronger, just as seeing the world through the eyes of the omniscient God makes us wiser."

Therefore, while many of us are called to a life of action, making the most of our unique talents and doing good works, it is wise continually to seek balance in our lives by nourishing our souls. It has been said that prayer precedes progress and power, and that God must work in us before he can work through us. By seeking a deeper personal union with God, we will draw strength and guidance for the journey, and we will be assured that we are on the right path.

That it will never come again is what makes life so sweet.

Emily Dickinson

Enjoy the little things in life, for one day you may look back and realize they were the big things.

Anonymous

To stop praying is to take a wrong turn, because prayer is the door through which all of God's graces come to us.

St. Theresa of Avila

A day hemmed in prayer is less likely to become unraveled.

Anonymous

My secret is very simple. I pray.

Mother Teresa

24
HOW TO TAKE MEASURED RISKS

The future belongs to those
who believe in the beauty of their dreams.
Eleanor Roosevelt

Have you ever looked at an ancient map? Do you recall seeing a picture of a ferocious dragon on one side of the map or the other? According to Roger Von Oech, an author and creativity consultant, when ancient mapmakers wanted to chart something beyond the known world, they would sometimes draw a picture of a dragon, signifying danger. If an explorer wanted to enter this unknown territory, he would be placing himself—and his men—at risk. Some explorers were frightened by the symbol; others saw it as an opportunity, a chance to discover something new, maybe a chance to get rich.

In a sense, each of us has a mental map by which we guide ourselves from day to day. Like ancient maps, our mental maps might also have dragons signifying areas that we feel are off limits. Sometimes these dragons are valid and important warnings that keep us from danger. Sometimes, however, they merely prevent us from making the most of our talents and learning something new; they hold us back from some of the riches that life has to offer.

We have seen how it is wise to strike a balance between rest and work, prayer and action. In the same way, it is wise to strike a balance between safety and growth, security and the realization of our potential.

Life, to be sure, is difficult and fraught with uncertainty. Socially, politically, and economically, we live in a perilous age; we sense that the earth may give way beneath our feet and that we will tumble down a bluff and into a sea of turmoil where we will scarcely be able to manage the strong currents and keep our head above the cold, dark swells. Even with regard to our personal lives, we recognize that there are many things beyond our control, that there are no guarantees that our efforts will yield the results that we desire. Thus we sometimes seek to build a refuge of security in which we can safely reside.

There is no doubt that this is important, to a degree, especially if we have a family to protect. But the thicker the walls we build to protect ourselves from life, the greater the chance that those same walls may also prevent us from living; in securing ourselves against the winds of fortune, we may also be tying ourselves down and making it difficult or impossible to move forward toward growth and maturity.

Therefore, it is important to find a balance between safety and living our lives fully. "One does not discover new lands without consenting to lose sight of the shore for a very long time," wrote André Gide. Indeed, we must be willing to take risks, to leave the safe and familiar, if we are to become what we are capable of becoming. Though we should be careful not to put ourselves or our loved ones in unnecessary jeopardy; though our decisions and pursuits should always be in accordance with our means and capabilities; though our voyage across the sea of life should be well planned, and we should use the best instruments of navigation at our disposal and stock our vessel with the necessary provisions for our well-being and survival, we still must be willing to leave port and set sail over unknown waters for the destination of our greatest talents, for the distant shore of our dearest dreams. There is no doubt that there will be times when the passage is difficult, when we are stranded in the doldrums or violently tossed by strong winds and ominous seas, but this is the price we must pay for growth and fulfillment, for living our lives fully.

Determine that the thing can and shall be done,
and then find a way.

Abraham Lincoln

Feed your faith and your doubts will starve to death.

Anonymous

Be always a little bit afraid
so that you never have need of being much afraid.

French Proverb

Who goes for a day in the forest should take bread for a week.

Czech Proverb

The marvelous richness of human experience would lose
something of rewarding joy if there were no limitations to overcome.
The hilltop hour would not be half so wonderful
if there were no dark valleys to traverse.

Helen Keller

25
MAKING A LIVING, MAKING A LIFE

We make a living by what we get;
we make a life by what we give.
Arthur Ashe

Some people are fortunate in that they can make a secure living while they are making use of their greatest talents. But many of us have to balance the development of our most cherished talents with the more practical necessities of life. For example, you might want to become a doctor or a university professor, and this might take many years of study before you can begin to make a living from your talents. Or perhaps you want to start a business, and this means giving up the safety and security of another career. Or perhaps you wish to become an artist or a writer, and you know that it might be difficult to provide for yourself while making use of these God-given talents.

Something that you might find helpful is to remember that you probably have an array of talents, some of which may be more practical than others. For example, although my dream and calling is to write books like the one you are reading now, I also work as a business consultant and business writer. In addition, I've bought and renovated a number of older homes, selling them for a profit. After all, the artist must eat. If you have a family, the stakes are even higher.

One of Aesop's fables hit me right between the eyes when I first read it. It's about a magnificent stag that goes down to a pond for a drink of water. As he bends over the surface, he sees his own reflection, and he is struck by the beauty of his majestic antlers. At the same time, he sees his skinny, bony legs and feels contempt.

Later that day, the stag is grazing in a field when he sees a lion quietly stalking him from the tall grass. Instantly he flees, and the lion gives chase. The stag is so fast that he is able to outrun the lion, gaining a comfortable distance. But as he enters a wooded area, his antlers get stuck in the branches of some trees. The lion catches up and pounces on him with teeth and claws.

"Woe is me!" thinks the stag, just before dying. "I despised my skinny legs, which might have saved my life, and I revered my glorious antlers, which ended up bringing about my demise."

You almost certainly have some glorious, God-given talents that you are called to develop and share with the world, but don't lose sight of the fact that God has probably also given you some practical talents and abilities to carry you on your life's journey. "All work that uplifts humanity has dignity and importance and should be undertaken with painstaking excellence," said Martin Luther King, Jr. Your more practical talents will help you balance security with growth, safety with taking risks.

In everything you do, put God first, and He will direct you
and crown your efforts with success.

Proverbs 3:6

Soon after the death of Rabbi Moshe, Rabbi Mendel of Kotz asked
one of his disciples: "What was most important to your teacher?"
The disciple thought and then replied:
"Whatever he happened to be doing at the moment."

Hasidic Tale

We do not need to carry out grand things in order to show great love for God and for our neighbor. It is the intensity of love we put into our gestures that makes them into something beautiful for God.

Mother Teresa

Our grand business is not to see what lies dimly at a distance,
but to do what lies clearly at hand.

Thomas Carlyle

You never know what you can do until you try.

English Proverb

26
THE TREASURE OF YOUR TIME

This is the day which the Lord hath made, let us rejoice and be glad in it.
Psalms 118:24

In one of his novels, Dostoyevsky tells the story of a man who has been sentenced to death. The man is led to the gallows where he is to be executed, and a priest comes to hear his last confession. He has only a few more minutes to live. But then, just before the sentence is to be carried out, he is given a reprieve and is condemned to another punishment instead.

These few minutes, when he thinks that death is imminent, seem to him "like an infinite time, a vast wealth." But "nothing is so dreadful as the continual thought, 'What if I were not to die! What if I could go back to life, what eternity! And it would all be mine! I would turn every minute into an age; I would lose nothing, I would count every minute as it passed, I would not waste one!'"

The incident, which is based on Dostoyevsky's own reprieve after he had been sentenced to be executed by a firing squad, affirms how we can truly come to value life when we are in fear of losing it. Prior to this, it is easy to get lost in a world of trivial urgencies and petty concerns, to let the minutes and hours slip by without a thought for their irretrievability and worth. In fact, sometimes the demands of the day and the unspoken pressures of our age can be so overbearing that we feel quite unhappy and maybe even despise our lives.

But consider for a moment, if you were sentenced to die, if you had only a few more minutes or hours or days to live, how would you then feel about your life? And what, in retrospect, would you wish you could do differently? Your answers should determine the way that you now live.

In truth, we are all sentenced to death, and whether we part from this miraculous existence in five minutes or five years or fifty, our time is brief and should be guarded and used with great love and care. "The hour that gives us life begins to take it away," said Seneca. "Like as waves make toward the pebbled shore, so do our minutes hasten to their end," wrote Shakespeare.

Death limits our existence, but it also helps give it meaning; for if we had an eternity on this planet to work out our problems, to realize our talents and potential, then there would be no urgency or reason to act now rather than later, and our days and weeks would be stripped of much of their purpose and value.

It has been suggested that in moments of quiet contemplation, we regard our lives, and those who are a part of our lives, as though we have already lost them to death, only to retrieve them back for a little while. This, in effect, is the experience of Dostoyevsky's prisoner, and such reflection makes us profoundly aware of the value of the passing minutes and hours of our existence, as well as of the value of our family and friends and the importance of their respective happiness and well-being. We do not have an eternity to work out our problems, to realize our potential, to live our lives fully. We must begin now, or our resolve weakens, our energy diminishes, and doing so becomes increasingly difficult and unlikely. Our lives are the sum of the passing hours and days that we often so carelessly throw away. We are prone to kill time when we should strive to make it live.

If you would, ask yourself: How many more sunsets will I be able to see? How many more walks on the beach or in the mountains will I be able to take? How many more times will I be able to hold my wife or husband or children in my arms? How many more days will I have to pursue my dreams, to live my life fully?

"Work while it is called today," wrote Benjamin Franklin, "for you know not how much you may be hindered tomorrow. One today is worth two tomorrows; never leave until tomorrow that which you can do today."

The same imperative might be given to love, forgive, pray, enjoy, experience, learn, and laugh.

It is the wisest who grieve most at the loss of time.

Dante

Short as life is, we make it still shorter by the careless waste of time.

Victor Hugo

You waste the treasure of your time.

William Shakespeare

You should live your life as if you are ready to say good-bye to it at any moment, as if the time left you is some pleasant surprise.

Marcus Aurelius

Dost thou love life?
Then do not squander time,
for that is the stuff of which life is made.

Benjamin Franklin

27
SEIZE THE MOMENT

You may delay, but time will not.

Benjamin Franklin

Each of us has a unique contribution to make to the world, to life. Never before has a person been born with precisely your characteristics, with your blend of experiences, values, and talents. Never before has anyone had your distinct vision of a better world. These differences, the things that make each person unique, are also what make each indispensable and irreplaceable. Only you can fulfill your destiny and make your vision a reality.

It is impossible to tell a person what path he should follow, and those who would do so, who would try to influence and control the lives of their children or others beyond sympathetic encouragement and loving support, are doing them a disservice. Only you, in stillness and humility, can listen to the dictates of the still small voice that guides you, perhaps not all at once, but slowly, tenderly, to your most satisfying path. Only you can sense what direction your life must take in order to fulfill your highest destiny, and only you can find the will and discipline to follow this path with all your strength and all your heart.

It fills one with courage to think that we are almost always free to start again. Regardless of what wrong turn we might have taken, we can, from this moment, resolve to live the life we have glimpsed in moments of blessed inspiration, developing our special talents, enjoying the wonders of existence, making our life a gift to the world. Regardless of the mistakes we have made, the people we have hurt, the opportunities we have squandered, the time we have wasted, we can, from this moment, decide to make the most of our remaining days and years. "From the lowest depth there is a path to the loftiest height," wrote Carlyle.

But to follow this path requires that we focus on what is important, on what takes us closer to our goals, on what enables us to live our lives most fully, and to refrain, as far as possible, from spending time on what is not important. Our days have become terribly busy and complicated. We live in a hurried age, full of restlessness, noise, and activity. Rushing this way and that, taking care of the many demands and urgencies that press upon us, we exhaust our energies and are dismayed to see that little of worth actually gets accomplished. "Paralyzed by a thousand and one considerations, we never get to the point of allowing free play to whatever greatness may be burgeoning within us," said Goethe.

A great deal of what we do can be replaced, if we choose, by activities that exercise our greater talents and abilities, that take us closer to our dreams. It is a matter of being conscious of our time and using it effectively. We may ask ourselves, at moments throughout the day, "Is what I am doing or about to do truly important? Does it express my greatest talents? Does it take me closer to my most cherished ideals? Is it the best contribution I can make to my job, my family, to the world in which I live?" If the answer is no, and if we have the freedom to do the greater thing, then we must seize the moment and do so. "Our lives are frittered away by detail," said Thoreau; he counseled that we strive for "simplicity and elevation of purpose." La Rochefoucauld warned, "Those who give too much attention to trifling things become generally incapable of great ones."

The great thing that we decide to pursue will become the distant star by which we navigate our life. Perhaps we are called to grow and blossom where we are, to honor our commitments and responsibilities by doing better and more conscientious work in the place of our employment, by being a more loving and empathic parent, child, or spouse. Perhaps we have a special dream or talent that must be developed and pursued if we are to fulfill our highest destiny. Only you can determine your path, and it is your foremost challenge to do so. Then you must do what you can to simplify your life so that you can direct as much precious time and energy as possible to your goal. "As a gardener by severe pruning forces the sap of the tree into one or two vigorous limbs, so should you stop off your miscellaneous activity and concentrate your force on one or a few points," advised Emerson.

You cannot ride in all directions at the same time.

Yiddish Proverb

He who would arrive at the appointed end must follow a single road and not wander through many ways.

Seneca

One day Alice came to a fork in the road and saw a chesire cat in a tree. "Which road do I take?" she asked. His response was a question: "Where do you want to go?" "I don't know," Alice answered. "Then," said the cat, "it doesn't matter."

Lewis Carroll

No wind serves him who addresses his voyage to no certain port.

Michel de Montaigne

Greatness of soul consists not so much in soaring high and in pressing forward, as in knowing how to adapt and limit oneself.

Michel de Montaigne

28
STAND ON THE SHOULDERS OF GIANTS

In all things, success depends upon previous preparation,
and without such preparation
there is sure to be failure.

Confucius

Although your strength lies in originality, and although your purpose must come from the depths of your being, there is much that you can learn from those who have come before you. Over two centuries ago, the artist Sir Joshua Reynolds gave a series of lectures at Oxford University on the nature of creativity and the development of the artist. While stressing the importance of originality, he said that the daily food and nourishment of the artist should be the great works of his predecessors. In studying and contemplating these works of genius, the artist is warmed by their contact and captures their spirit of excellence and simplicity. Furthermore, he combines what he has learned from studying these masterpieces with his own experience of nature and life and comes up with new forms and patterns. "Invention, strictly speaking," said Reynolds, "is little more than a new combination of those images which have been previously gathered and deposited in memory. Nothing can be made of nothing; he who has laid up no materials can produce no combinations."

Many of the most inventive and ingenious figures of the ages have stressed the importance of education, of preparation, and they have acknowledged the debt they felt to those who came before them. "If I have seen further it is by standing on the shoulders of giants," said Isaac Newton. "The roots of education are bitter, but its fruit is sweet," commented Aristotle. Albert Einstein acknowledged, "Many times a day I realize how much my own outer and inner life is built upon the labors of my fellow men, both living and dead, and how earnestly I must exert myself in order to give in return as much as I have received." Louis Pasteur noted, "In the field of observation, chance favors the prepared mind."

Preparation is indispensable to progress. Regardless of the specific path we have chosen, we can learn from others who have also turned their backs on mediocrity and conformity and set forth for the glorious peaks of their highest abilities and aspirations. Although our path will at some point diverge from theirs, we can draw strength and encouragement from their example and learn from their achievements and mistakes. In many cases, they have charted maps and chronicled the difficulties that we may encounter on our journey; they have climbed to the heights of their respective destinies and described for us what they have seen. "To know the road ahead, ask those who are coming back," says a Chinese proverb.

Take a moment to consider, "Who can help me with my journey? Who has passed this way before?" If this person is still living and if it is possible to make contact, make it your goal to do so, perhaps with a brief and respectful letter. Not everyone will be receptive, but some people want to help others when their schedules permit. It is simply another way for them to express their unique talents, to do their part of the world's work.

Once a boy was in his backyard, trying to lift a heavy stone. He pushed and pulled and worked up a sweat, but he could not move it.

His father passed by and said, "Son, are you doing all that you can to lift that stone?"

The boy was frustrated. "Yes, of course I am!"

"No you're not," the father said, rolling up his sleeves. "You haven't asked me to help."

Asking for help and guidance can sometimes be a key that opens doorways of opportunity. In addition to trying to contact people who might help you, you can also stand on the shoulders of giants by procuring a helpful book from your local library or bookstore. "A book is the precious lifeblood of a master spirit," wrote John Milton. In a few hours of reading, in quiet companionship across time and space, you may stumble upon an idea that changes your life; you may also find the inspiration you need to move beyond discouragement and fear. Others have surmounted great difficulties in pursuing their dreams. Drawing strength from their example, you can, too.

A field, however fertile,
cannot be fruitful without cultivation;
neither can a mind without learning.

Cicero

He who is afraid of asking is afraid of learning.

Dutch Proverb

No one knows less than he who knows it all.

American Proverb

Learning is a treasure that follows its owner everywhere.

Chinese Proverb

Books are nourishment to the mind.

Italian Proverb

29
FOUR WORDS THAT CAN TRANSFORM YOUR LIFE

New day, new fate.

Russian Proverb

Your journey to the summit of your talents begins where you are, with a single step. "Small opportunities are often the beginning of great enterprises," said Demonsthenes. "From a little spark may burst a mighty flame," said Dante.

Often we are reluctant to take this first step because we do not feel prepared; we want everything to be just right before we get started. But the truth is, things will never be just right, since we can always have relatively more time, energy, money, and knowledge before beginning than we now have. The question, therefore, is not what we would do if we had better means, but what will we do with the means that we have? Not what we would do if we had better opportunities, but what will we do with the opportunities at hand?

Centuries ago, according to a rather famous story, the Italian sculptor Donatello took delivery of a huge block of marble. After looking at it carefully, he rejected it as being flawed. He said that it had too many cracks and imperfections.

His contemporary, Michelangelo, took a look at the same piece of marble. He, too, noticed its imperfections, but he saw it as a challenge to his skills as an artist. So he accepted the block of marble that Donatello had rejected, and he proceeded to carve from it one of the masterpieces of the ages: the statue of David.

Some people let their imperfect situations hold them back. Rather than rolling up their sleeves and making the best of what they have, they focus on what they are lacking; they focus on "the cracks in the marble." Others, however, know that they cannot wait for everything to be perfect and that they must make the best of their situation. They know that if there's a magic key to success, it's forged in the fires of hard work and attention to detail; they know that if there is a path to success, it is taken one small step at a time.

Our golden opportunity, the thing that will lead us upward, is often right before us; it might be a simple and common task, perhaps part of the responsibilities of our day; it might be something we know in our hearts that God is calling us to do. It may not be a giant leap, but it is a step, and if we do it well, to the best of our ability, it will lead us upward to the next step, and to the next. "Our grand business is not to see what lies dimly at a distance, but to do what lies clearly at hand," advised Thomas Carlyle. "Practice yourself, for heaven's sake, in little things; and thence proceed to greater," said Epictetus. "Slight not what is near through aiming at what is far," wrote Euripides.

Mother Teresa once told Father Benedict Groeschel that if she had not picked up the first dying man off the streets of Calcutta, then she and the Missionaries of Charity would not have helped hundreds of thousands of others. Her ministry began with a single step, a single act of compassion, a simple "yes" to what God was calling her to do at that moment. She had the courage to start, and then to keep going. "From small beginnings can come great things," says a proverb. What simple step can you take today? How can you say *yes*?

Even though there are many things that lie outside our sphere of influence and control, to a significant degree, we shape our lives by the decisions we make, by the actions we take. At any given moment, on any given day, there are many things that we can choose to do. One of these things we decide upon and make a permanent part of our lives and a permanent part of the world in which we live. In this way, we shape and are responsible for our own destiny, as well as the destiny of mankind. In this lies our greatest freedom, our most awesome responsibility.

Therefore, consider this day to be a fresh start. Know that your future does not have to equal your past. The direction in which you are moving is all that matters now. Yesterday is gone;

you can't get it back, and dwelling on it will only interfere with your ability to make today and the rest of your life a masterpiece. Seize the moment and concentrate on the one thing you can do that will set you on the right path. If the story of your life has been less than exemplary, write a sentence today that sets it off in another direction, changing tragedy to triumph, fear to faith, and lost opportunity to loving action. Add another sentence tomorrow, and so forth, until you have created a life story worthy of your extraordinary potential. In this sense, the words "new day, new fate" can transform your life.

Often we are afraid to take this first step. We sense that there will be heartache and pain on the road ahead; we fear that our dreams will be shattered, that we will stumble and look foolish. It is with good reason that we have such fears. Life is difficult; there will certainly be troubles on the road ahead; there will certainly be pain as we test our ideals against reality, as we try to find our way. But in acting, in taking our first step, and then the next, we arrive at the higher realization that life is not only conflict and tribulation, but that it can also be victory, transcendence, and growth. In acting, in being willing to endure pain in order to experience joy, we open our eyes and see the splendid colors and textures of life; we open our ears and hear its beautiful harmonies and rhythms; we taste its bitterness, but we also experience its sweetness.

Whatever you do or dream you can do—begin it.
Boldness has genius and power and magic in it.

Goethe

You must do the things you think you cannot do.

Eleanor Roosevelt

Lord, grant that I may always desire more than I can accomplish.

Michelangelo

It is a rough road that leads to the heights of greatness.

Seneca

What lies behind us, and what lies before us,
are tiny matters compared to what lies within us.

Ralph Waldo Emerson

30
BE AN INSTRUMENT OF PEACE

There is no situation that cannot be ennobled by achievement or enduring.

Goethe

The moments of our lives are irreplaceable and invaluable. Each opportunity to add to the quality of our existence, to choose growth and the expression of our talents, is taken or lost forever. It is how we seize the passing moment, how we make use of the day, that ultimately determines the quality and direction of our lives. Today is the necessary product of our yesterdays; our tomorrows are shaped by how we live today. We must therefore find the courage to take the first step, and then the next, so that we can make our way to our highest destiny. In so doing we will have given ourselves momentum, however slight, and we will have turned our backs on mediocrity and conformity to face the radiant white peaks of our greatest potential. "Press on," wrote Victor Hugo. "A better fate awaits you."

But what if something holds us back, something that is beyond our control—a debilitating illness, for example, or a cruel and oppressive environment from which we cannot possibly get free? We have already seen how difficult it is to move forward in life if we are suffering through a personal crisis or a loss of confidence and faith. The best we can do, at times like these, is to cope with the demands of daily living, to gradually learn the lessons of our suffering, and to heal, to become whole again. But what if our crisis is so severe, so harsh, that healing and freedom are impossible? What if that which holds us back is something we cannot change, regardless of our strength, determination, and patience—something we can only endure?

Viktor Frankl has written at length about his nightmarish experiences in the Nazi death camps. At Auschwitz, he faced horrors that words cannot adequately describe: hunger, cold, lack of sleep, exhausting work, physical and mental torture, the constant threat of death. Yet even under these hellish conditions, men and women were able to give their lives meaning, says Frankl; they were able to choose the way in which they endured their suffering: "We who lived in the concentration camps can remember the men who walked through the huts comforting others, giving away their last piece of bread. They may have been few in number, but they offer sufficient proof that everything can be taken away from a man but one thing: this last of human freedoms—to choose one's attitude in any given set of circumstances, to choose one's own way."

Sigmund Freud believed that if a group of people faced starvation, all of their individual differences would disappear and they would be motivated solely by their need to survive. Thank heaven Freud was not a prisoner in the concentration camps, says Frankl; but if he had been, he would have seen that this is not true. Frankl recalls men and women whose "behavior in the camp, whose suffering and death, bore witness to the fact that the last inner freedom cannot be lost. The way they bore their suffering was a genuine inner achievement. It is this spiritual freedom that cannot be taken away which makes life meaningful and purposeful."

In this lies the most significant meaning of the Parable of the Talents, for it also applies to what we do with our spiritual gifts and talents. When we make use of our spiritual gifts, when we choose, prayerfully and with God's help, to be instruments of peace, even in the face of difficult or impossible circumstances, then we find that our lives take on a new sense of purpose and meaning. Other measures of success become superficial, for the person we become is the ultimate measure of success.

"There are victories of the soul and spirit," wrote Elie Wiesel, another Holocaust survivor. "Sometimes, even if you lose, you win." Victor Frankl remarks, "We may find meaning in life even when confronted with a hopeless situation, when facing a fate that cannot be changed. For what then matters is to transform a personal tragedy into a triumph, to turn one's predicament into a human achievement. When we are no longer able to change a situation . . . we are challenged to change ourselves."

Long ago, in a land faraway, there lived a king who owned the most beautiful diamond in the world. It was radiant, almost as if someone had captured the brightest ray of sunlight and put it inside a beautifully shaped gem.

One day, by accident, the diamond sustained a deep scratch. The king was very upset. He called in the most skilled artisans in the region, and he offered them a great reward if they could remove the scratch and restore the beauty of his most treasured possession. But the artisans all said that there was nothing they could do.

Some time later, a wise man came to the king and promised that he could make the diamond even more beautiful than it had been before the accident. The king was a bit skeptical, but impressed by the man's confidence, he entrusted him with his precious stone.

The wise man kept his promise. With beautiful artistry and care, he engraved a lovely rosebud at the tip of the imperfection, and he used the scratch to make a stem.

Teach me the way I should go, for to you I lift up my soul.
Psalms 143:8

*We must learn to endure what we cannot avoid.
Our life is composed, like the harmony of the world,
of contrary things, also of different tones,
sweet and harsh, sharp and flat, soft and loud.
If a musician liked only one kind, what would he have to say?
He must know how to use them together and blend them.*
Michel de Montaigne

*In the depth of winter,
I finally learned that within me lies an invincible summer.*
Albert Camus

*God grant me the serenity
to accept the things I cannot change,
the courage to change the things I can,
and the wisdom to know the difference.*
Reinhold Niebuhr

I asked God for strength that I might achieve;
I was made weak that I might humbly learn to obey.
I asked for help that I might do greater things;
I was given infirmity that I might do better things.
I asked for riches that I might be happy;
I was given poverty that I might be wise.
I asked for power that I might have the praise of men;
I was given weakness that I might feel the need of God.
I asked for all things that I might enjoy life;
I was given life that I might enjoy all things.
I got nothing that I asked for, but everything
I hoped for; almost despite myself my
unspoken prayers were answered.
I among all men am most richly blessed.

Prayer of an Anonymous Civil War Soldier

31
THE PERSON YOU BECOME

Everything that happens to us leaves some trace behind; everything contributes imperceptibly to make us what we are.
Goethe

Thankfully, most of us are not victims of such harsh and impossible circumstances as those described in the previous chapter. We are not terminally ill or incapacitated; we are not victims of man's frightening capacity for evil. Instead, we are relatively free to pursue our dreams, to find creative work that makes use of our unique talents and abilities. However, the person we become is still of paramount importance. The way we perform our work and relate to others still shapes our character and spiritual life. We create our work, and our work creates us. This truth is expressed in the world's great religions and philosophies. "What you are is the sum of everything you have said and done," said the Buddha. "Our characters are the result of our conduct," commented Aristotle. "Our acts make or mar us; we are the children of our own deeds," wrote Victor Hugo.

Unfortunately, many of us are more concerned with external measures of success than with peace of mind and personal integrity. Often we measure our progress and worth by the money we make, by the possessions we accumulate. Sometimes, like Tolstoy's Ivan Ilyich, we are willing to ignore the dictates of our conscience in order to achieve these material ends. But as Jesus admonished, what does it profit a person to gain the world if he loses his soul? Of what worth are external riches if we suffer from internal poverty?

Regardless of where we are, regardless of what we do, the tasks and responsibilities before us, the challenges of the day, are of vital importance to our spiritual growth and integrity. At the core of our being, we somehow know the truth about ourselves, and we suffer when we do things superficially, when we do less than we are paid for or less than we can expect of ourselves. Each slighted responsibility, each poorly performed task, diminishes our sense of worth and self- respect. We lose faith in ourselves, in our powers, and in our own goodness. "The deeds of a person become his life, become his fate," wrote Tolstoy. "This is the law of our life."

Doing our best, however, working with love, giving rather than taking, makes us feel whole; kindness, generosity, and honesty are reflected in our spirit rather than selfishness or dishonesty. For this reason, if we do not feel compelled to give our best, if we are not currently trying to express our highest talents and abilities, then it would perhaps be better to change positions, to get in a place that calls out our deeper affections. "It is not what we do but how much love we put into it," said Mother Teresa. "Work is love made visible," wrote Kahlil Gibran. "And if you cannot work with love but only with distaste, it is better that you should leave your work and sit at the gate of the temple and take alms of those who work with joy. For if you bake bread with indifference, you bake a bitter bread that feeds but half a man's hunger. And if you grudge the crushing of the grapes, your grudge distills a poison into the wine."

According to a tale told by William Bennett, centuries ago, a famous sculptor was laboring over a block of stone. He chiseled and carved and polished with the utmost care, as he sought to turn the stone into a thing of beauty.

"Why are you spending so much time and effort on that section?" someone asked him in passing. "It's going to sit fifty feet high, supporting the roof. Nobody is going to see or know that you've done such a fine job."

The venerable artist paused from his work and said, "But God will see, and I will know."

It does not matter so much what you do,
what matters is whether your soul is harmed by what you do.
If your soul is harmed, something irreparable happens,
the extent of which you won't realize until it will be too late.

Albert Schweitzer

Do what you reprove yourself for not doing.
Know that you are neither satisfied nor dissatisfied
with yourself without reason.

Henry David Thoreau

Don't leave the high road for a shortcut.

Portuguese Proverb

A clear conscience is a good pillow.

French Proverb

I care not so much what I am to others as what I am to myself.

Michel de Montaigne

32
THE POWER OF PATIENCE

How poor are they that have not patience!
William Shakespeare

Nothing of value can be accomplished in this world without love, hard work, and sacrifice. The greater your dream, the more you expect of yourself, the more you are called by God to do, the more discipline and strength it will take you to reach your goals. "Long is the road from conception to completion," said Molière. "Those who aim at great deeds must also suffer greatly," observed Plutarch.

Unfortunately, we live in an age when people expect things to happen instantly; in fact, it is considered a virtue if we can do things easily and get immediate results, if we can become an "overnight success." In a sense, we have lost touch with the rhythm of the earth, with the march of the seasons. We mistakenly expect to throw some seeds on the ground and to have them yield an immediate and abundant harvest. We forget that the fields must be carefully tilled and cultivated; that the seeds we sow must be nourished and cared for with the water of hope and the sunlight of love and faith; that we must have the patience to wait for them to grow, blossom, and come to fruition. “The greatest secret of life is to know how to wait,” said one wise soul.

Part of the problem stems perhaps from the public’s fascination with those who get rich quickly. Another factor could be that we live at a time in which commerce and technology are largely concerned with finding ways to do things faster and with greater ease. Many of us have embraced this appetite for expediency and convenience; rather than focusing on the development and expression of our talents and on the results we wish to achieve, we concentrate on finding easy and pleasing methods. The results do not matter so long as we can get by without too much effort. This is a mistake. When we observe those who fulfill their talents and abilities, who realize their ideals, we see that they look beyond comfortable and pleasing methods and focus on the goal they wish to achieve. They willingly give up a safe and easy path and instead focus on the distant peaks of their highest dreams and aspirations. Then, with patience and determination, they find or forge a trail to get there.

It has been said that genius is the infinite capacity for taking pains, and many of the most creative spirits who have walked this earth would humbly agree. “If I have done the public any service,” commented Sir Isaac Newton, “it is due to patient thought.” “Let me tell you the secret that has led me to my goal," said Louis Pasteur: "My strength lies solely in my tenacity." Albert Einstein observed, "I think and think for months and years. Ninety-nine times, the conclusion is false. The hundredth time I am right."

In the arts, too, excellence is achieved through hard work, patience, and persistence. "God sells us all things at the price of labor," said Leonardo da Vinci. "The best of me is diligence," wrote Shakespeare. "Work is my chief pleasure," said Mozart. Charles Dickens commented, "My own invention or imagination, such as it is, I can most truthfully assure you, would never have served me as it has but for the commonplace, humble, patient, daily, toiling, drudging attention." And Montesquieu, speaking of one of his writings, said, "You will read it in a few hours, but I assure you that it has cost me so much labor that it has whitened my hair."

Being patient by working hard and striving for excellence is important, and so is being patient by focusing on one small success at a time. There is a wonderful Egyptian folktale, which can be traced back to Aesop and which is adapted here from a retelling by Inea Bushnaq, about a poor boy who, when he comes of age, sets out to make his fortune. With borrowed money he buys several hundred freshly laid eggs and carefully places them in a large round basket. Then he boards a small boat that is sailing down the river to Cairo.

As the boat glides down the river, the boy stretches out in the sun and begins to daydream. "When I get to Cairo, I will go to the market and sell my eggs. Then, with my profit, I will buy some fine cloth and bring it back to my village. The women there will crowd around me and buy the material to sew clothing for their families. With my profits, I will pay back my creditors and buy a ewe. I will take good care of her and she will give birth to two lambs. I will then sell the ewe and the lambs and buy a cow. When the cow gives birth to a calf, I will sell them both and have enough money to hire a servant. Then I will be able to say, 'Do this! Do that! Go here! Go there!' And if he disobeys, I will kick him in the pants, like this . . ."

Caught up in his daydream, the boy accidentally kicks his basket of eggs, sending it into the Nile. The eggs disappear in an instant, and he is left with nothing.

Patience is bitter, but its fruit is sweet.

Jean-Jacques Rousseau

Have patience and the mulberry leaf will become satin.

Spanish Proverb

Even the highest tower begins from the ground.

Chinese proverb

The person who built a castle
is the one who put one stone in place at a time.

Italian Proverb

They who like things to be easy will have difficulties;
they who like problems will succeed.

Chinese Proverb

33
BUILD A BRIDGE TO YOUR DREAMS

Fortune favors the bold.
Latin Proverb

In pursuing our dreams, in developing our talents, it is inevitable that we will run up against obstacles that try our faith and test the limits of our endurance. At times, it has been observed, as we climb to our personal summit it appears that our path is blocked and that further progress will be impossible; dismayed, we might believe that we have traveled far and suffered much for naught. But if we have the courage to continue, there is a chance that we will get closer and see that the path is not actually blocked, but that it stretches gently around a corner and continues on to our goal. "I find nothing so singular in life as this," said Nathaniel Hawthorne, "that everything opposing appears to lose its substance the moment one actually grapples with it."

At other times, however, our path does indeed lead to a dead-end or is blocked by some obstruction that seems truly insurmountable. These are the moments that test our will and determination, that call out our strength of spirit. Sometimes we can chisel away at the boulder that blocks our path, finding a way over or around it; sometimes, however, we have to retreat and reflect on the merits of our pursuit ("One must often step back in order to make a better leap," says a Danish proverb). If we decide to press on, then we will have to find or make another path that will lead us to our goal.

Aesop illustrates the importance of persistence in his fable of the lion and the gnat. "Get away from me, you little pest!" says the lion to the gnat. The gnat is offended and immediately declares war. "Do you think I'm impressed or frightened because they call you king?" challenges the insect. "The ox is stronger than you, and I can make him do my bidding at the slightest sting!"

The gnat charges into battle, pouncing on the lion's back and driving him mad with irritation. The lion is so enraged that other creatures in the area take cover. The tiny bug torments and stings him in a hundred places, on the back, on his face, and finally, up his nose. The agony!

The lion tears at his own flesh, trying to get rid of the annoyance. At last, exhausted by rage, the king of the jungle collapses. The victorious gnat, beaming in glory, retires from the fight as he entered it, blowing his own horn. But as he buzzes around, boasting of his victory, he runs into a spider's web. And that is the end of him.

Like the gnat, we, too, can triumph over giant obstacles

and overwhelming circumstances by stinging in a hundred places, by breaking our problems into manageable pieces and then tackling these pieces one at a time. However, also like the gnat, in escaping one danger we can sometimes fall prey to another. We must therefore stay in the present, focused on the task at hand.

Breaking our problems into manageable tasks, dividing and conquering, can help us achieve extraordinary things over time. If you've ever had a chance to visit the Golden Gate Bridge in San Francisco, you know that it is one of the most amazing things ever built. Two enormous steel cables, each over a mile long, and each suspended from two 746-foot towers, hold up the roadway, which is crossed by millions of vehicles each year. These cables are a little over three feet in diameter, and because they weigh over 24 million pounds each, they could not be installed all at once. There was no way to manufacture them on the ground, raise them into the air, and place them in the saddles atop the two main towers.

So how did the cables get there? Well, each cable is actually made up of 27,572 individual wires, each about as thick as a pencil. These wires were put in place and then workers bound them together to make sixty-one separate strands. Then the strands were compacted under enormous pressure and bound together to make the three-foot cables. Once compacted, workers wrapped the cables with a fine wire to give them a smooth finish.

So the giant cables that support tens of millions of pounds of weight were actually created one small wire at a time. In a similar way, if you faithfully discharge one small task and achieve one small goal at a time, these will add up and carry a lot of weight in your life. Like the smaller wires that make up the giant cables of the Golden Gate Bridge, your smaller triumphs will combine to support you as you seek to realize your potential and create a special life. They will build a bridge to your dreams.

Difficulties give way to diligence.
German Proverb

Diligence is the mother of good fortune.
Miguel de Cervantes

You have to accept whatever comes and the only important thing is that you meet it with the best you have to give.

Eleanor Roosevelt

Perseverance is a great element of success.
If you only knock long enough and loud enough at the gate,
you are sure to wake up somebody.

Henry Wadsworth Longfellow

Life affords no higher pleasure than that of surmounting difficulties, passing from one step of success to another, forming new wishes, and seeing them gratified.

Samuel Johnson

34
RISE EVERY TIME YOU FALL

Our greatest glory is not in never falling,
but in rising every time we fall.
Confucius

From 1968 to 1972, the United States sent nine manned spaceships to the moon. Six of these landed on the surface, carrying out a variety of experiments in such locations as the Sea of Tranquillity and the Ocean of Storms. Their crews brought back hundreds of pounds of lunar rocks and dust for scientific testing. Other experiments were carried out in space. Hundreds of new products and technologies were developed as a result of the magnificent endeavor. Perhaps most important, people worldwide witnessed and marveled at what humans can achieve when working together and setting lofty goals.

One mission, however, is remembered less for its scientific achievements than for the way its astronauts and ground crew responded to adversity. On April 11, 1970, three astronauts were transported to a launch pad, where they took an elevator 363 feet to the top of a Saturn 5 rocket. They climbed into a small command module, were strapped in, and prepared themselves for take off. They were the astronauts of *Apollo 13*.

At 1:13 P.M., 1313 in military time, the countdown

started and the engines of the rocket were ignited. Flames shot downward, and the earth trembled. Moments later, the Saturn 5 rocket carrying the Apollo 13 command module, a smaller lunar module in the front, and a service module in the rear, roared into the sky. It was scheduled to reach the moon's gravitational pull on April 13.

All space missions have their share of challenges and glitches. The astronauts and mission control specialists are highly intelligent and highly trained; they are able to handle most of these challenges calmly and creatively. They have the "right stuff."

A little less than three minutes into the *Apollo 13* mission, the first stage of the Saturn 5 rocket was jettisoned. The astronauts felt the thrust of the five second-stage engines being ignited, but something went wrong. A warning light indicated that the center engine hadn't ignited.

The astronauts waited to hear whether Mission Control would abort their mission. Instead, after a few moments, they were told that they would reach space with the remaining four engines burning longer than normal. "Looks like we've had our glitch for this mission," one of the astronauts quipped.

The next two days went almost perfectly; in fact, it was considered one of the smoothest flights in the history of the program. Someone in Mission Control even joked that they were "getting bored to tears down here."

Then on the evening of the third day, 200,000 miles away from the earth—four fifths of the way to the moon—one of the spacecraft's oxygen tanks exploded, causing the second tank to leak too. A "Crew Alert" warning light went on; the spacecraft shook and careened from side to side. "Houston, we have a problem," one of the astronauts said, as they tried to get the craft under control.

Indeed, they faced a number of serious problems. To begin with, they had only fifteen minutes of life support left in the command module. This meant that they would have to quickly move to the lunar module at the front of the spacecraft. The lunar module had its own life support and power supplies, but it was designed for two astronauts rather than three, and for about a day and a half of flight. They were at least three or four days from earth.

Also, because it had thin walls and no heat shield, the lunar module would never be able to enter the earth's atmosphere. Consequently, they had to shut down the command module to preserve some of its power and oxygen for reentry into the earth's atmosphere. If they ever made it back to earth, they would reenter the command module and try to power up this "mother ship" again.

Mission Control decided that the only way to get the astronauts back to earth was to have them circle the moon and use its gravity to "slingshot" the spacecraft back toward earth. If they made an error—if the thrusters were not fired just right—they could be as many as 40,000 miles off course, shooting past the earth and into space. Fortunately, however, their calculations were correct. The command module's thrusters fired just right and they were on their way home.

But the astronauts encountered a number of other problems. To begin with, because they were running with very little power, the temperature in the lunar module was almost freezing, and the astronauts also suffered from a lack of food and water. One of them got very sick; all were exhausted from not sleeping. Also, an alarm went off and they realized that the carbon dioxide levels were rising dangerously, as a result of their own breathing, because the lunar module's air filters had clogged up. They would die if this problem was not solved.

Fortunately, Mission Control had anticipated this and figured out a way for the astronauts to put together and attach a makeshift air filter, using cardboard, socks, plastic bags, tape, and other things they could find in the spacecraft. This worked.

In addition, no one knew whether they would be able to restart the almost frozen command module after it had been shut down. This was new territory, and they needed to succeed in order to reenter the earth's atmosphere. Fortunately, after some tense moments, they were able to power it up.

Nearing earth, they had to jettison both the service module in the back of the spacecraft and the lunar module in the front, which had been their "lifeboat" for almost four days. As the service module drifted away, the astronauts noticed that the explosion had torn away pieces of its side. Were pieces missing from the command module, too? Were there holes in the heat shield and would the craft burn up when it entered the earth's atmosphere? They would know in minutes.

The world waited, watched, and listened as *Apollo 13* neared the earth. As it entered the atmosphere, radio contact was lost for about four minutes. Then, from a recovery ship in the South Pacific, people saw a tiny silver object falling to earth. Two large orange parachutes opened and the spacecraft gently touched down in the ocean. Minutes later, helicopters were hovering over it. Divers opened its hatch and the astronauts were lifted from the sea.

What can we learn from this story? To begin with, human beings are remarkably creative and resilient when it comes to facing adversity, and you can be, too. If you doubt this, bear in mind that you come from a long line of survivors. Your ancestors, going back many thousands of years, were able to face the rigors of life, and you have survived and most likely prospered thus far, too.

Second, you *will* encounter obstacles. Almost every mission has its glitches. This is the way things are. But getting knocked down doesn't mean getting knocked out. It simply means that you need to make some adjustments in your approach; it means that you try something new, with all the knowledge and experience gained from your first effort. In this sense, we all fail our way to success.

Finally, even after you experience adversity and setbacks, you have to go on believing in yourself and trying to make the most of your God-given talents and abilities. After the *Apollo 13* mission, *Apollos 14, 15, 16*, and *17* all touched down on the moon. The space program didn't fold up; people didn't cower and say, "We can't do this." They made improvements and pressed on, and since then, we've continued to explore space through the space shuttle and other programs.

NASA called *Apollo 13* a "successful failure" because of the extraordinary way that people worked as a team to rescue the crew. There were many heroes who showed great courage, resourcefulness, and resolve. Tapping your "right stuff," you too can make successes of your failures.

We become brave by doing brave acts.

Aristotle

Failures are the pillars of success.

Latin Proverb

Much of the good that might have been achieved in the world is lost through hesitation, faltering, wavering, vacillating, or just not sticking with it.

William Bennett

The greater the difficulty, the more glory in surmounting it. Skillful pilots gain their reputations in storms and tempests.

Epicurus

If you can force your heart and nerve and sinew
To serve your turn long after they are gone,
And so hold on when there is nothing in you
Except the Will which says to them, "Hold on!" . . .
Yours is the Earth and everything that's in it,
And—which is more—you'll be a Man, my son!

Rudyard Kipling

35
HOW TO TAP YOUR EXTRAORDINARY POTENTIAL

That is what I am, God's pencil. A tiny bit of pencil with which He writes what He likes. God writes through us, and however imperfect instruments we may be, He writes beautifully.

Mother Teresa

In the Parable of the Talents, the reward for work well done is more work. "You have shown that you are trustworthy in handling small things, so now I will trust you with greater," said the master to his worthy servants. They who have much, who find and make use of their talents, discover that they have even more to do. As they find the courage to take action, their abilities grow; as their abilities grow, so do their dreams and aspirations. Their lives are full, rewarding, satisfying. But those who hide their talents, who succumb to laziness, fears, or false values, forfeit even the little bit of satisfaction they once had. Their lives become stagnant, dark, boring. They have progressively less purpose and satisfaction.

It is in working, in developing our talents and pursuing our dreams, that we participate in life and tap our extraordinary potential. "Work is the inevitable condition of human life, the true source of human welfare," wrote Tolstoy. Indeed, if we are alive, if we can still draw breath and are reasonably aware of our talents and capabilities, then there is more we can do, there is more we must do, if our lives are to go on having purpose and meaning, joy and satisfaction. "Life never ceases to put new questions to us," said Viktor Frankl. We are as young as our responsiveness to these questions, as old as our unwillingness to hear; we are as young as our faith, hope, and love; as old as our doubts, fears, and indifference.

There is so much that is wrong in the world, so much unnecessary pain, suffering, cruelty, and injustice. We know this, and where we know it, we can take steps to alleviate it. We have seen human beings at their best, in moments of beauty and compassion, helping those less fortunate, relieving suffering, comforting the needy and afflicted, striving to make this world a better and safer place. We have enjoyed the fruits of their labor; the beautiful music and art that took years of hard training to produce; the great literature and ideas that required a lifetime to discover and express; the many products and services that sustain us and that bring joy into our lives, thanks to the courage and hard work of the people who produce them. We have seen and experienced what is highest in human nature, and we know that a better world is possible.

The greatest danger in life lies in losing our sensitivity, our reverence for life and for the world in which we live. In our youth we are often idealistic; we are full of passion for good and feel indignity for the injustices of the world. As we get older, however, we notice that some of the people around us have lost some of their compassion and sympathy. Maybe this is the way, we think, and we start to let our own values slide. We decide that the world is indeed a hard place and that the best we can do is to protect ourselves, to get all we can, and not to worry too much about others.

This is a dangerous path that leads away from the clear and spectacular mountaintops, past the concrete world of mere conformity, to a wretched swamp from which it is difficult to get free. We can rationalize that we are animal in nature, that it is natural to compete, that the strong survive and prosper while the weak suffer and perish. In part this is true; nature is amoral, and we are part of nature. But what distinguishes humans, what makes us different from rodents and reptiles, is our consciousness of the value of life, our compassion for other living things, our capacity for love, kindness, and altruism. It is in fulfilling these qualities that we live the life that is most distinctly human, that will lead to our fullest and most complete development and satisfaction.

Each of us, where we stand, can picture a better world and

know our place in it. Whether it is being a good parent, friend, or employee; whether it is developing our special talents or pursuing our greatest dreams, there is something that each of us can do within our sphere of influence. The scope of what we do is not important. We have only to fulfill the tasks and responsibilities before us, to do the best we can, where we are, with what we have. A person "has not everything to do, but something," counseled Thoreau.

It is interesting that, immediately following the Parable of the Talents in the Gospel of Matthew, Jesus places great emphasis on small, seemingly ordinary acts of kindness and love. He tells how in giving a hungry person something to eat, or a thirsty person something to drink, we are also doing it for him. "Truly, I say to you, inasmuch as you have done it to the least of these my brothers, you have done it to me." The same is true when we visit the sick or lonely, or when we help clothe or shelter those in need. These are small acts, like tiny brush strokes, but with God's help, they create a masterpiece of a life.

Therefore, we should not think that we have to do great things in order to fulfill God's plan for our lives. If he has given you a special talent and filled your heart with a special dream, then by all means, follow this path with all the faith and hope and love that you can muster—even though it may lead to times of difficulty. But as Mother Teresa once said, God does not necessarily call us to do great things, "He calls us to do small things with great love."

In utilizing our talents, in serving God and our fellow human beings, we each have the opportunity to participate more fully in life. This has been the lesson of many of the world's great religions and philosophies. In the Parable of the Talents, the master said, "Come and share in my happiness," to the servants who had the courage to use and multiply their talents. Perhaps God has given us each the chance to share in His happiness; perhaps we each have the opportunity to share in the joy, the exhilaration, the unparalleled fulfillment of helping to create the world in which we live.

Last night I thought in a dream that the shortest expression
of the meaning of life is this: the world moves, is being perfected;
it is man's task to contribute to this motion
and to submit to and cooperate with it.

Leo Tolstoy

Let us go forth to lead the land we love,
asking His blessing and His help,
but knowing that here on earth God's work must truly be our own.

John F. Kennedy

Human progress never rolls on the wheels of inevitability; it comes through the tireless efforts of men willing to be co-workers with God, and without this hard work, time itself becomes an ally of the forces of social stagnation. We must use time creatively, in the knowledge that the time is always right to do what is right.

Martin Luther King, Jr.

A man, after he has brushed off the dust and chips of his life, will have left only the hard, clean question: Was it good or was it evil? Have I done well—or ill?

John Steinbeck

If I can stop one heart from breaking,
I shall not live in vain;
If I can ease one life the aching,
Or cool one pain,
Or help one fainting robin
Unto his nest again,
I shall not live in vain.

Emily Dickinson

Part Two

The Path with Heart

36
DECIDE WHAT SUCCESS MEANS TO YOU

We are prone to judge success by the index of our salaries or the size of our automobiles rather than by the quality of our service and relationship to humanity.

Martin Luther King, Jr.

What is the meaning of success? For many of us, being successful means material and financial prosperity. How much money we make, the kind of car we drive, the size of the house we live in—all of these are considered important measures of how we are doing in life. To a large degree, we judge each other and, ultimately, ourselves by what we have rather than by what we are or what we do.

But is success truly a matter of what we possess and of how much money we make? Does a well-furnished house make our lives worthwhile? Does an expensive automobile give us a sense of well-being and fulfillment?

Experience and common sense tell us that, though money and property can be an important part of our lives, they do not necessarily make a person happy or at peace. Our hearts and souls can starve in the midst of all the money and material possessions in the world; our greatest individual potential can lie dormant and unexplored, weighted down by visions of silver and gold. What is more, some of the most successful people who have ever lived are people who often had little or no money: Mahatma Gandhi died possessing only a pair of sandals, a robe, a staff, a spinning wheel, his spectacles, and a prayer book. Mother Teresa possessed very little, too. Socrates cared more about a good conversation than about his next meal. Confucius was dependent on his small band of disciples. Rembrandt ended his life in austerity, as did Beethoven, Bach, and Van Gogh. Jesus died leaving only a robe for which the Roman soldiers cast lots.

None of these individuals was rich in a conventional sense. None of them had money or a large estate. Yet all of them, most would agree, lived great lives and were in their own way successful. Perhaps, then, success can mean more than just material and financial prosperity. Perhaps it is more than a matter of what we earn or possess.

I have an irrepressible desire to live until I can be assured that the world is a little better for my having lived in it.

Abraham Lincoln

It is not the brains that matter most, but that which guides them—
the character, the heart, generous qualities, progressive ideas.

Fyodor Dostoyevsky

How far that little candle throws his beams!
So shines a good deed in a naughty world.

William Shakespeare

He who wishes to secure the good of others
has already secured his own.

Confucius

Success

To laugh often and much; to win the respect of intelligent people
and the affection of children; to earn the appreciation of critics
and endure the betrayal of false friends; to appreciate beauty;
to find the best in others; to leave the world a bit better,
whether by a healthy child, a garden patch,
or a redeemed social condition; to know that even one life
has breathed easier because you have lived—this is to have success.

Ralph Waldo Emerson

37
WHAT YOU CAN LEARN FROM SOCRATES

The unexamined life is not worth living.
Socrates

Determining the meaning of success and the type of life we feel is most worth living is a difficult and personal affair. There are, to be sure, many ways to look at success, and no one definition is true to the extent that it excludes all others. Success can mean contentment, health, good familial and social relations, and the realization of our unique talents and abilities. It can also mean integrity, faith, and the ability to enjoy life in all its variety and splendor.

Trying to define success takes us from the realm of science, with its impartial methods and precise formulations, into the world of philosophy, which is more subjective and less conclusive. "The noblest of all studies," wrote Plato, "is the study of what man is and of what life he should live." This is philosophy's chief objective, and each individual who seeks the truth patiently, deliberately, and with an open mind is in effect a philosopher. The answers we seek are often elusive, but we are almost always blessed for our efforts with greater understanding and humility—in a word, with greater wisdom.

During his trial, Socrates told the Athenian court that the only reason he might be considered wiser than others was because he was profoundly aware of his own ignorance with regard to life's most important matters. Life and our place in it are indeed perplexing. Trying to solve the problems of existence, even deciding how we can best live, is something like trying to solve a puzzle that has seemingly infinite variables, some of which can only be assumed. It is more than our limited faculties of reason and perception can handle. It is often easier to go along with what others say is right and to conform to standards and values that may not truly be our own.

At times this means measuring the quality and worth of our lives in dollars and cents. Our progress is commonly determined by our paycheck, our value by our investments. But upon reflection, many would agree that money and property may in fact have very little to do with our sense of happiness and fulfillment. "The impression forces itself upon one that men measure by false standards," contended Sigmund Freud, "that everyone seeks power, success, riches for himself and admires others who attain them while undervaluing the truly precious things in life." Perhaps those whose lives are dominated by the pursuit of wealth will become disillusioned, feeling that the star by which they have navigated their lives has led nowhere and left them stranded on a sea of discontent. Perhaps they will die with the highest and most precious part of their nature largely undeveloped and unexpressed. It is therefore vital that we each examine the values by which we live, to decide what is truly important and what will ultimately give us feelings of fulfillment and well-being. Socrates' maxim that the unexamined life is not worth living is extreme, but at the very least the unexamined life is in danger of being misdirected and even wasted.

In every person there is something precious which is in no one else.
And so we should honor each for what is hidden in him.

Hasidic Saying

Towering genius disdains a beaten path.
It seeks regions hitherto unexplored. . . .
It thirsts for distinction; and, if possible, it will have it.

Abraham Lincoln

Gallantly, ceaselessly, one must fight for inner liberty.

Abraham Joshua Heschel

The principal effect of the power of custom is to seize
and ensnare us in such a way that it is hardly within our power
to get ourselves back out of its grip and return unto ourselves
to reflect and reason about its ordinances.

Michel de Montaigne

Thus to be independent of public opinion
is the first formal condition of achieving anything great
or rational whether in life or in science.

G. W. F. Hegel

38
HOW TO LIVE A CONTENTED LIFE

A person who sows seeds of kindness enjoys a perpetual harvest.

Anonymous

Through the years philosophers and writers have tried to define what in ethics is called "the good life," that is, the way in which we can best make use of our brief worldly existence. For Socrates, self-knowledge is the chief good. For Aristotle, it is realizing our full potential as rational beings. For the Stoics like Epictetus and Seneca, the good life is one of discipline, self-denial, and the development of character. Many of us today, however, would define the good life as being one of ease and comfort, wealth and plenty. The philosophers mentioned above, along with many others, would be highly critical of these values.

One system of thought that would support our quest for comfort and plenty is the ancient Greek philosophy of hedonism, which considers immediate pleasure to be the highest good in life. According to hedonism, humans by nature are pleasure-seeking animals, and each opportunity for pleasure must be enjoyed in the full lest the opportunity be gone forever. "Eat, drink, and be merry, for tomorrow we may die" is the ethic practiced by the hedonists, and it is an ethic adhered to by many today (although we will often forego an immediate pleasure for one we feel will be greater in the future). Having fun, retiring in luxury at an early age, grasping for all we can get—these goals are commonplace enough. Success for many of us is determined by what we can take or get, by how pleasant and comfortable we can make our lives.

This propensity toward pleasure is not hard to understand. Not only is it in our nature to seek pleasure and avoid pain, but people today are often plagued by a sense of vagueness and futility, a feeling of emptiness that they try to fill. Science has made us increasingly aware of the smallness of our position in the cosmos. Our little planet circles a star that is one of billions of stars in a galaxy that is just one of billions of galaxies in a universe that itself might be destined to decay and die. The history of our species (not to mention our own life spans) is but a blink in eternity. It seems that nothing we do, individually or collectively, can make much of a difference anyway.

Compounding our sense of futility is the threat of nuclear annihilation, the knowledge that life as we know it could be wiped out, perhaps because of an absurd dispute or misunderstanding. Or maybe our promising species could fall prey to a virus, a mindless strand of protein thousands of times smaller that the head of a pin but highly contagious and capable of ending our lives without the slightest remorse.

Given this pessimistic outlook and the insecurity it breeds, it is not surprising that many of us make pleasure our purpose, giving our desires free reign, taking as much as we can get when we can get it. However, a life filled with pleasure is not necessarily a life well lived. Neither, for that matter, is a life that makes power its chief aim, as we will see in the next chapter.

For a Contented Life

Health enough to make work a pleasure;
Wealth enough to support your needs;
Strength enough to battle with difficulties and overcome them;
Grace enough to confess your sins and forsake them;
Patience enough to toil until some good is accomplished;
Charity enough to see some good in your neighbor;
Love enough to move you to be useful and helpful to others;
Faith enough to make real the things of God;
Hope enough to remove all anxious fears concerning the future.

Goethe

He who likes things to be easy will have difficulties;
he who likes problems will succeed.

Chinese Proverb

An aim in life is the only fortune worth finding.

Jacqueline Kennedy Onassis

An aspiration is a joy forever,
a possession as solid as a landed estate,
a fortune which we can never exhaust and
which gives us year by year
a revenue of pleasurable activity.

Robert Louis Stevenson

39
TAKING CARE OF YOUR SOUL

The interior joy we feel when we have done a good deed,
when we feel we have been needed somewhere
and have lent a helping hand, is the nourishment the soul requires.
Albert Schweitzer

Some people believe that power is the most important component of a "good life." This point of view, foreseen but not advocated by Plato in the fourth century before Christ, has as its most articulate and passionate spokesman the nineteenth-century philosopher Friedrich Nietzsche. Living amidst the changes in perspective brought on by Darwinism, Nietzsche saw the will to power as the underlying motive behind people's actions and the uninhibited realization of the will to power as the greatest good to which one can aspire. To be powerful is to prosper and survive, to be weak is to suffer and perish. Morality, said Nietzche, begins as a set of arbitrary rules invented by the weak "herd" to protect itself from strong individuals. Religion is morality taken to an extreme, with God's will and the threat of eternal punishment as its mandate. Nietzsche despised religion, especially Judaism and Christianity, because it teaches compassion and preserves the weak, inhibiting what he believed to be the natural advancement of mankind.

Nietzsche's perspective is shocking and disturbing, but the sentiment that people are by nature selfish creatures interested foremost in their own survival and well-being is commonplace, as is the sentiment that being powerful leads to greater levels of happiness and success. But does power truly make us feel successful, or like pleasure, does it still leave something missing in our lives?

Compared to much of the world, the majority of people in the United States and other Western democracies already live pleasurable lives and have a great deal of power. There is, to be sure, a dreadful amount of poverty and want, even in developed countries, but most of us are fortunate enough to have good food to eat, warm beds to sleep in, clothes to wear. Music, entertainment, and other pleasures are plentiful. In comparison with the richest king of medieval times—even of a hundred years ago—many of us have remarkable luxuries and opportunities. Television, radio, computers, and telephones are things that we take for granted. Cashing our paycheck and walking into the nearest supermarket or department store is like having the goods of thousands of specialized servants at our disposal. Buses, subways, and cars can take us places faster than a team of horses. We can even fly. Medical science and hygienic improvements have practically doubled our life expectancy and the survival rate of our children. But still, as rich and powerful as we are, we want more. Many of us do not feel successful and we struggle to understand the sense of emptiness and alienation that sometimes permeates our lives.

What is the cause of our discontent? What can we do that will make us feel that our lives are more meaningful and worthwhile? The answer has been given by the great writers, thinkers, and spiritual leaders of each generation, but it seems to get lost in the constant shuffle and petty exigencies of our daily lives. At times, in our strident efforts to keep abreast of the fast pace and competitive nature of our modern world, we lose sight of what is truly important. We forget that true success is multifaceted, involving our all-around development as human beings. It is not only a question of what we can get or receive, but also of what we give. It is growth, integrity, friendship, faith, and love, and these do not come so much from what we possess as from the pursuit of a worthy purpose, from making ourselves a worthwhile part of the world in which we live.

Each time anyone comes in contact with us,
they must become different
and better people because of having met us.
We must radiate God's love.

Mother Teresa

*Miss no single opportunity for making some small sacrifice,
here by a smiling look, there by a kindly word;
always doing the smallest thing right and doing it all for love.*
St. Thérèse of Lisieux

*The future of civilization depends on our
overcoming the meaninglessness and hopelessness
which characterizes the thought of people today.*
Albert Schweitzer

*You want to know how to overcome despair?
I will tell you. By helping others overcome despair.*
Elie Wiesel

To ease another's heartache is to forget one's own.
Abraham Lincoln

40
LIGHT ONE SMALL CANDLE

It is better to light one small candle than to curse the darkness.

Confucius

Albert Schweitzer, the Nobel Peace Prize laureate who spent fifty years of his life serving his fellow human beings in the oppressive heat of the African jungle, providing medical aid to those most desperately in need, said, "I don't know what your destiny will be, but one thing I do know: the only ones among you who will be really happy are those who have sought and found how to serve."

Leo Tolstoy wrote, "Life is a place of service, and in that service one has to suffer a great deal that is hard to bear, but more often to experience a great deal of joy. But that joy can be real only if people look upon their life as a service, and have a definite object outside themselves and their personal happiness."

Martin Luther King, Jr., observed, "Every man must decide whether he will walk in the light of creative altruism or in the darkness of destructive selfishness. This is the judgment. Life's most urgent question is, what are you doing for others?"

And Albert Einstein, in an article in which he tried to define success, wrote, "Only a life lived for others is a life worthwhile."

The importance of giving, the path to a greater sense of success and fulfillment, is also a central lesson of the world's great religions. "They who give have all things," says a Hindu proverb, "they who withhold have nothing." In the Buddhist scriptures it is written, "The man of wisdom who did good, the man of morals who gave gifts, in this world and the next one too, they will advance to happiness." In the Koran, Mohammed conveys that "a man's true wealth is the good he does in this world." In the Torah it is written that the Lord gives to "every man according to his ways, according to the fruit of his doings." And in Christianity we learn that "it is more blessed to give than to receive" and that "he who is greatest among you shall be your servant."

Indeed, none of us has a chance of living a great life, of continually fulfilling his or her highest needs and potentialities, except those who have looked for and found a way to serve. The great people of history, those who have earned our respect and admiration, those whom we can truly call successful, are people who have in some way enriched the lives of their fellow human beings. Whether it is Shakespeare, Bach, Monet, Mother Teresa, or Martin Luther King, Jr., what is remembered and cherished is not how much money they made or how large a house they lived in, but how their works help us enjoy and understand our world; what is celebrated is not the power they held, but how in expressing what was highest and most noble in their natures they help us experience what is most exalted in our own.

One does not have to compose a symphony to live a great life; nor does one have to paint a masterpiece or write a work that becomes a classic. All of us, where we are, can make our work a gift to the world. A parent raising children, a teacher inspiring students, a business-person providing excellent service—no matter where we are, we can do something to add to the quality of life of those around us. The opportunity to do so is right before you, in the thing you are about to do.

In making our work and daily actions a gift to the world, in making them an expression of our love for life, for God, and for others, we fulfill our highest potential, our most beautiful destiny as human beings. In lighting one small candle of kindness and truth, we do our part to overcome some of the world's darkness and despair.

I long to accomplish a great and noble task, but it is my chief duty to accomplish humble tasks as though they were great and noble. The world is moved along, not only by the mighty shoves of its heroes, but also by the aggregate of the tiny pushes of each honest worker.

Helen Keller

No energy is lost in the world,
nor is it merely the souls of men that are immortal
but all their actions as well. They live on through their effects.
Goethe

Do not pursue spectacular deeds. What matters is the gift of yourself,
the degree of love that you put into each one of your actions.
Mother Teresa

It does not matter whether you achieve much or little,
provided your heart is directed to Heaven.
The Talmud

No work is insignificant. All labor that uplifts humanity has dignity and importance and should be undertaken with painstaking excellence. If a man is called to be a street sweeper, he should sweep streets even as Michelangelo painted, or Beethoven composed music, or Shakespeare wrote poetry. He should sweep streets so well that all the host of heaven and earth will pause to say, "Here lived a great street sweeper who did his job well."
Martin Luther King, Jr.

41
ONE WORD THAT WILL GIVE YOU THE FREEDOM TO SUCCEED

Our life is frittered away by detail. . . . Simplicity, simplicity, simplicity, I say! Simplicity of life and elevation of purpose.
Henry David Thoreau

Why do some of us get sidetracked into "lives of quiet desperation"? The answer, as we have seen, lies at least in part in our pursuit of what William James, in a letter to H. G. Wells, called "the bitch-goddess success"—our society's "squalid cash interpretation" of the word "success," which, he said, "is our national disease." But is money really so bad? Is it truly the root of all evil? Is it to blame if our lives are not as fulfilling and meaningful as they might be?

Not money but the love of money, the pursuit of money to the exclusion of other worthy aims, is the root of our malady. Money itself is benign; it is merely a medium of exchange by which we trade the fruits of our labor for the products and services of others. As such, it is necessary for our very survival. With money, we indirectly exchange the goods and services we produce for food, shelter, and clothing; it pays for books, tuition, and medical bills; in some cases, it can even save lives.

"If money go before, all ways do lie open," said Shakespeare.

Indeed, money can act like a lubricant that helps us move through life with greater ease and comfort, with less friction. It enables us to rest when we are tired or weary, it can give us the time and resources we need to cultivate our minds and our talents. Lack of money, on the other hand, can make our lives painfully cumbersome and difficult. Our options and our sense of freedom become limited; sometimes we have to take a job that we don't particularly like or acquiesce to terms that others dictate just in order to survive ("My poverty, but not my will, consents," to quote Shakespeare again). Moreover, when we are constantly preoccupied with our next meal or with a stack of unpaid bills, it becomes difficult, if not impossible, to pursue our higher aspirations and more worthy goals. "Ready money works great cures," says a French proverb. "Save money and money will save you," says an English proverb. "The heaviest burden is an empty pocket," observes a Czech proverb.

Money, therefore, is not the great evil; it is, in fact, a necessary part of our complicated lives in today's world. But if we make money our life's purpose, our reason for being, then we may be ruining our chances for a greater sense of success and fulfillment. "Money is a good servant, but a bad master," said the English philosopher Francis Bacon. The path we should take is thus a matter of personal reflection and judgment. The question of money, like so many other issues in philosophy and life, does not resolve itself neatly into black and white, right and wrong. It is incumbent on each of us to examine his or her life and to come up with a personal, sensible, and moderate approach to money—what Aristotle would call the Golden Mean and what in Confucianism is called the Doctrine of the Mean. For many of us, this moderate approach will lead to greater simplicity, which can give us the freedom we need to pursue our dreams and aspirations.

If you have money, you are wise and good-looking
and you can sing well, too.

Yiddish Proverb

Money talks, and it usually says "good-bye."

Anonymous

If you would be rich in a year, you may be hanged in six months.

Italian Proverb

God helps the poor: he protects them from expensive sins.

Yiddish Proverb

Getting money is like digging with a needle;
spending money is like water soaking into sand.

Japanese Proverb

42
CONSIDER THE COST OF WEALTH

There is no greatness where there is not simplicity, goodness, and truth.

Leo Tolstoy

But following a moderate course and striving for greater simplicity will never be easy. If you are like many people, a part of your nature will always pull you in another direction, that of conforming to the standards of the world rather than the eternal truths of your soul.

Tolstoy illustrates this challenge in his haunting story "How Much Land Does a Man Need?" The story is about a peasant whose goal in life is to own more and more land. He already owns a farm of considerable size, but it is not enough and he wants more. When he hears that the government is practically giving away as much land as a person can claim in another part of the country, to promote that region's growth, the peasant takes temporary leave of his family and makes the long journey to seek his fortune.

When he gets there he learns the rules of the transaction: he must begin at a specified point at sunrise and run or walk as far and as wide as he can by sunset. All of the land within the borders he traverses will be his so long as he gets back before sundown. If he fails to get back on time, he gets no land and he does not get another chance to stake a claim.

The peasant is thrilled at the opportunity. He rests that night the best he can, and the next morning, as the first sliver of the sun peeks over the horizon, he gets his turn and sets out at a steady pace so as to conserve his energy. He starts by walking briskly north so that he can watch the ascending sun to his right. After going a long way in this direction, he thinks that it would be prudent to turn east. But the land is so rich and fertile that he simply must have more, so he goes just a little bit farther to broaden his claim.

Finally, he drives a stake into the ground, turns east, and starts off in that direction. The sun is blazing hot now and he is covered with perspiration. His legs are heavy, but his ambition carries him forward. No longer able to see the place where he started, he again thinks it would be wise to turn and start in the next direction, but the land is too beautiful, he must own it, so he goes just a little bit farther before driving in another stake.

When he does turn south, his mouth is parched and his lungs ache. He feels that he cannot go on, but something inside pushes him forward. After today he will have plenty of time to rest.

The sun is descending as he turns west, on the last leg of his journey. The place where he started is still just a speck on the horizon; it will be a race for him to get back before the deadline. He lumbers forward, barely able to lift his legs. At last he can make out the place where he started and the faces of the people there. They are laughing at him.

The sun sinks heavy and orange; just a few seconds more. The tired peasant struggles to the finish line and falls over just as the last rays of the sun disappear over the horizon. He's made it. The land is his. But his victory is short-lived, for on the spot he collapses of exhaustion and dies.

What a tragic parable this is for our times. People everywhere are in a race for more land, more money, a bigger house, a better car. In many cases they run themselves into the grave, barely stopping to enjoy the simple pleasures in life and to appreciate the many comforts that they already have. To paraphrase an English proverb, many people spend their health acquiring wealth, and then spend their wealth trying to regain their health.

In light of this story, you might ask yourself, "Am I running at a frantic pace? Am I enjoying the many riches that I already have—my health, my relationships, the simple joys of life, the beauty and splendors of this earth? When I am older and look back on my life, how will I wish I had lived?"

Most of the luxuries and many of the so-called comforts
of life are not only not indispensable,
but positive hindrances to the elevation of mankind.
Henry David Thoreau

In character, in manner, in style, in all things,
the supreme excellence is simplicity.
Henry Wadsworth Longfellow

Possessions, outward success, publicity, luxury—
to me these things have always been contemptible.
I believe that a simple and unassuming manner of life is best
for everyone, best for both the body and the mind.
Albert Einstein

Paralyzed by a thousand and one considerations,
we never get to the point of allowing free play
to whatever greatness may be burgeoning within us.
Goethe

Are you not ashamed of your eagerness to possess the greatest amount of money and honor and reputation, while you do not care for or give thought to wisdom and truth and improvement of your soul?

Socrates

43
GIVE YOUR HEART TO THINGS THAT MATTER

Moderate riches will carry you;
if you have more, you must carry them.
English Proverb

According to a fable by Aesop, a little boy once reached into a jar for a handful of nuts. He grabbed as many nuts as he could, but he was unable to get his hand back out of the jar—the neck was too narrow for his fist. He tried and tried again, and at last he began to cry.

"What's wrong?" said his mother, who heard the commotion from another room.

"I can't get the nuts out of this jar," the boy cried.

"Well, why don't you be less greedy? Just take a few at a time, and then you'll find that you can get your hand out of the jar."

The boy tried this and discovered that his mother was right. "Why didn't I think of that?" he said.

Many people today get stuck in an unpleasant situation because they are trying to grab too much too fast. Why is this? What causes us to want money and property and to want them now?

To begin with, there is doubtless something in our genetic makeup that accounts for our acquisitiveness, our desire for property and material possessions. Other living things also have a tendency to build a nest or home, to protect it tenaciously, to stock it with provisions, and then to add to its store. Squirrels stow away nuts and berries; the family dog hides a bone; an ant struggles with a prize twig or morsel of food several times its own size, lifting, pushing, and dragging it back to what one hopes is a hero's welcome on the hill; a bumblebee diligently passes from one flower to the next, collecting more and more pollen before finally retiring to the hive.

In all of nature, even down to the cellular and microcellular level, those who survive are those who are able to fend for themselves and their families, protecting their territory and securing food and other necessities. Perhaps this explains, at least in part, the human compulsion for acquiring property and possessions: as with the ant and bumblebee, there could be something deep in our nature that compels us to build a home, to seek provisions, and then, when we have them, to go out and seek more (sometimes we even try to carry more than we can comfortably afford). Our predecessors who did not have these instincts simply did not survive.

Much of human behavior is learned, however, and to the biological impetus we can presently add others which are cultural in nature. To begin with, those of us in the United States are heirs to a legacy of frontierism. Our ancestors who came to this land from all parts of the world often left severe repression and austerity (with the exception of our African American ancestors, who were brought here cruelly against their will). They came in search of opportunity and fortune; often they were willing to endure significant hardships in order to build a better life for themselves and their families.

Once here, the new Americans built great cities and rapidly pushed from east to west, always seeking a new frontier, a new opportunity for wealth and prosperity. Along the way, they were sometimes blinded by their ambition, committing terrible atrocities: African slaves were bought and sold like animals and forced to build the fortunes of their white captors; an entire race of Native Americans was virtually exterminated and the land soaked with innocent blood; the advent of the Industrial Revolution began the sometimes mindless exploitation and irreparable damage of the nation's air, water, and precious natural resources. However, despite hardships and struggles, people were fascinated by the stories of those who made it, of those who struck it rich, and this fed the fire of frontierism.

Today, this spirit of frontierism endures; in a figurative sense, Americans are still pushing west, riding toward the proverbial sunset of more land, more money, more and better material possessions. We are still fascinated with stories of those who succeed, for if they have done it, surely we can, too. But when success is not immediately forthcoming, when the soil we till does not yield a quick harvest, many of us become frustrated and anxious. We look for a new frontier, but today's opportunities seem increasingly specialized and technical—they may require years of hard work and preparation. Sometimes an individual (or a group of individuals) feels that there is no way left for him to make it, that the American promise of abundance has been broken, that the dream is a lie. Sometimes he gives up or, worse yet, quiets his ambition and native restlessness in drink or drugs; sometimes the tension is even released in the form of crime and antisocial behavior—he strikes back at those who have misled him; he breaks the rules for which he feels contempt.

The tension many feel, the hunger for material and financial success, is heightened by the fact that our marketplace is crowded with all manner of products and luxuries, some of which are very useful, but some of which are, to quote Thoreau, "not only not indispensable, but positive hindrances to the elevation of mankind." We often think that we need the latest in fashion, cars, and appliances because we are persuaded, through clever advertising and promotion, to think this way. In reality, we may be just as happy, if not happier, without them, or at least with something more simple. Certainly, we would have more freedom to pursue our higher ideals if we were not spending our precious time and energy earning enough money to follow the latest trend.

As we will see shortly, one way to get out of this difficult situation—one way to get your hand unstuck from the jar—is to simplify your life and grab for less. Another way is to be aware of the many riches you already possess. Aside from material comforts, consider your health, relationships, the many things you've learned and accomplished.

A wise person once said that the way we can tell whether we are rich is not by how much money we have, but by how many things we have for which we would not take money. With this in mind, how much is being able to see a sunset or snow falling worth to you? For what would you trade your ability to listen to the sound of ocean waves or a child's laughter? How much money would you take for your ability to touch and hold the ones you love? How much is it worth to be able to think and reason and dream? What is the value of your freedom, your faith?

I think that a person who is attached to riches,
who lives in worry of riches, is actually very poor.
Mother Teresa

A good name is more desirable than great riches;
to be esteemed is better than silver or gold.
Proverbs 22:1

Lives based on having are less free
than lives based either on doing or being.
William James

He who is taught to live upon little owes more to his father's wisdom
than he who has a great deal left him does to his father's care.
William Penn

Civilization, in the real sense of the term,
consists not in the multiplication
but in the deliberate and voluntary restriction of wants.
This alone promotes happiness and contentment,
and increases the capacity for service.
Mahatma Gandhi

44
THE KEY TO GENIUS

Courage is the price that Life exacts for granting peace.
Amelia Earhart

So alluring is the treadmill of consumerism that we often judge our success by what we own or can buy. Money and possessions are something tangible by which we have come to measure the progress and value of our lives; a way of keeping score, if you will, a way of assessing our worth.

To be sure, it is necessary to make a living, and money and material possessions are essential to our well being and survival. What is more, it is natural and good to feel a sense of accomplishment and pride in taking care of ourselves and our families, in being rewarded for our service. Yet sometimes our pursuit of material success can cross a line and become single-minded and unrelenting. Moreover, it seems that few people have the courage and self-knowledge to do without such external rewards and to follow their own cherished vision, their own standard of excellence.

Vincent van Gogh sold only one painting in his entire career and was dependent on the generous but limited support of his brother. Still, he went on working and pursuing excellence;

sometimes he would not eat for days so that he could afford to buy more paints and canvases.

Walt Whitman sent his self-published book of poems, *Leaves of Grass,* to writers and literary critics across the country, hoping it would find acceptance. Instead, it was met with almost universal ridicule and rejection. His only solace was a note from Ralph Waldo Emerson, who encouraged him to keep writing, which of course he did.

Michelangelo lived a modest and solitary life with few luxuries and comforts. "Painting is my wife," he said; "my works are my children." Although he achieved a great deal of fame and served princes and popes, he focused intensely not on material rewards but on his development as an artist. "The promises of this world are for the most part vain phantoms," he said. "To confide in one's self and become something of worth and value is the best and safest course."

Such courage is as rare as genius. Many of us do not have a strong enough sense of purpose or identity to forego external rewards and to pursue our own idea of success. We put off developing our most cherished talents and push aside our youthful dreams to pursue something that seems more tangible and secure. Consequently, a part of our being remains unfulfilled. Only later in life, when we see that money and property cannot fill a lingering sense of emptiness, do we realize the magnitude of our mistake. Hopefully then we will attempt to truly live the precious days that remain by, as Simone de Beauvoir said, "pursuing ends that give our existence a meaning."

The richest man, whatever his lot,
is he who's content with what he's got.
Irish Proverb

None of those who have been raised to a loftier height
by riches and honors is really great.
Why then does he seem great to you?
It is because you are measuring the pedestal with the man.
Seneca

That which makes poverty a burden, makes riches also a burden.
It matters little whether you lay a sick man on a wooden
or a golden bed, for wherever he be moved,
he will carry his malady with him.
Seneca

Money may be the husk of many things, but not the kernel.
It brings you food, but not appetite; medicine, but not health;
acquaintances, but not friends; servants, but not faithfulness;
days of joy, but not peace or happiness.

Henrik Ibsen

When the game is over,
the king goes back in the sack just like the pawn.

Italian Proverb

45
THE FREEDOM OF SIMPLICITY

We should aim rather at leveling down our desires than leveling up our means.

Aristotle

Sometimes, if the success and riches that we seek are not immediately forthcoming, if the seeds we sow do not quickly grow to fruition, then we can create the appearance of success and enjoy prosperity before actually earning it. We can borrow money to buy the house or the car that we want; we can take out credit to purchase the right clothes and accessories. Although often useful, this can also be dangerous.

Americans are generally an impatient and restless people; especially in this age of push-button technology, we are used to things being fast and easy. Credit enables us to have what we want *right now,* without the pain of having to work and wait for what could be months or years.

We are also an optimistic people, and this native optimism can be both our strength and our downfall. We expect the best for ourselves, and rightly so. Often we will get the raise that we anticipate; often our investments will pay off. But after we have borrowed against these anticipated earnings, we sometimes find that our golden tomorrow brings its own needs and desires. The car for which we took out a loan now needs repair; the clothes we bought on credit are worn and out of style. Thus we may go on borrowing and buying, trying to quench our unending thirst for more and better, lugging behind us a load of debts.

These debts can have a paralyzing effect on our independence to pursue our higher ideals, on our ability to live successful and fulfilling lives. Credit can give us greater freedom and opportunity now, but down the line we may pay for this freedom and opportunity with compound interest. It may no longer be possible for us to change careers or to take a risk and pursue our life's dream because we need the money we are earning just to cover our bills. It may be difficult to take time off for health or personal reasons because we need to keep working to pay for what we have already used up, eaten, and worn out.

A number of proverbs warn about the pitfalls of going into debt. "Nothing seems expensive on credit," says one. "He who goes a-borrowing goes a-sorrowing," says another. "Our debts eat with us from the same dish," says another. A Latvian proverb notes, "It is better to go to bed on an empty stomach than to rise with debts." And a French proverb observes, "He is rich enough who owes nothing."

Of course, credit and debt are not all bad; like money, they have their good side and are an integral part of our lives in contemporary society. Credit can enable us to invest in the home of our dreams, the place where we feel we can create the best environment to raise our family; it can enable us to start a business and to bring a valuable product or service to the marketplace; it can help us take advantage of an opportunity which we feel may never occur again; it can get us through a difficult time or an emergency to which we might otherwise succumb. Like money, credit can be both a blessing and a curse. It is largely a question of our judgment in using it.

How then can we employ good judgment with regard to money and credit? The key, put simply, is to diminish our wants. Our basic needs for food, shelter, and clothing are relatively simple and easy to procure, but, as Epicurus wrote, "The wealth of vain fancies recedes to infinity." No matter how hard we try, no matter how much we struggle, we will always be one step behind our desire for more. Our freedom and contentment, therefore, lie in curbing our unlimited wants, rather than in trying to fulfill them, which is impossible. "It is not the man who has little, but the man who craves more, that is poor," said Seneca. "A man is rich in proportion to the number of things which he can afford to let alone," wrote Thoreau. "He will always be a slave who does not know how to live upon a little," stated Horace.

Upon reflection, most of us already have everything that can be enjoyed by the richest person in the world. We can sleep in only one bed, under one roof, at a time; we can wear one set of clothes, drive one car, and eat one meal at a time. Having a mansion with dozens of rooms, closets full of clothes, and a driveway lined with cars is really superfluous. All these possessions may make us feel secure, but true security comes not from what we own, which can always be lost, stolen, or worn out, but from confidence in who we are and in what we can do. Superfluous possessions may win us the respect and admiration of others, but such respect is often shallow and opportunistic, and such admiration is sometimes nothing more than smiling envy.

Moreover, filling our lives with property and possessions can actually take away our freedom to fulfill our higher needs. When we own something—a house, a car, whatever—it also owns a piece of us, proportionate to the importance we assign it in our lives. If we value property, then that property takes up a space in our heart, acting like a sponge and soaking up the love and passion that we could be channeling toward growth and more creative pursuits.

It is therefore imperative that we keep our wants within reason, curbing our natural propensity to hoard and collect, seeking a moderate course born of careful and independent thought, so that we can be free to develop our most cherished talents, so that we can give our heart to things that matter. We purchase our material possessions with money, but we purchase our money with our time and energy—in a word, with our lives. Indirectly, therefore, you are purchasing your property and material possessions with your life. It is up to you to decide whether you are paying too much or whether the transaction is just.

Too many people spend money they haven't earned,
to buy things they don't want, to impress people they don't like.
Will Rogers

Our luxuries are always masquerading as necessities.
French Proverb

Beware of little expenses; a small leak will sink a great ship.
Benjamin Franklin

As the wallet grows, so do the needs.
Yiddish Proverb

The pursuit of wealth, while natural and harmless in itself,
can carry serious spiritual dangers.
One way of testing whether our priorities are correct
is to get in the habit of speaking to God in prayer
about the things we want.
If we take prayer seriously and really open ourselves . . .
we'll find that our desires and wishes will be directed into channels
that are truly nurturing and healthy.

Jimmy Carter

46
BE GRATEFUL FOR WHAT YOU HAVE

A thankful heart is not only the greatest virtue,
but the parent of all other virtues.

Cicero

According to a folktale, adapted here from a version by Frances Jenkins Olcott, a young mother was once in the forest picking berries with her little daughter, whom she adored. Suddenly, as they made their way up the side of a mountain, the rocks parted before them and the entrance to a cave appeared.

A fairy dressed in a radiant white robe beckoned them to enter the cave. "Come here, young woman," she said, "see the riches that are inside. I will not harm you."

The young mother could see that the cave was filled with thousands of gold coins, piled everywhere and spread across the floor. "Take all of the gold you can grasp at once," said the fairy. "It will be yours to keep."

The young woman took her child by the hand and entered the cave. She stooped and picked up a handful of golden coins and put them in her pocket. Then, releasing her daughter's hand, she grabbed even more gold with both hands, and quickly rushed from the cave.

As she left, she heard the wall of the cave begin to close behind her, and the fairy said, "Foolish woman, you have lost your daughter for the sake of gold. Come back in exactly one year, and you will see her again." And then the door disappeared, as if it had never existed

"What have I done?" cried the mother. She tried desperately to get back inside, but to no avail. She beat her fists against the mountain wall and fell to the ground in anguish.

Exactly a year later, the young mother returned. The door to the cave was wide open, and the fairy sat at its entrance. Next to her stood the woman's daughter, who jumped for joy and yelled, "Mother, mother!"

"Come in," said the fairy, "and take all the gold coins you can grasp at once."

But this time the young woman only rushed for her daughter, taking the child in her arms and covering her with kisses.

"I don't want your gold," she said, "I only want my precious child."

This fairy tale is tragically relevant to our times, when many of us are so busy pursuing material success that we sometimes lose touch with the riches that we already have, namely, our relationships with family and friends. Certainly we all need to make ends meet financially, and making money is necessary and important, but we are each challenged to somehow, thoughtfully and consistently, balance making a living with making a life.

Another touching story, told for centuries in Eastern Europe and adapted here from a retelling by William Bennett in *The Moral Compass,* brings these ideas to life. Years ago, according to this folktale, a young man and woman fell in love and decided to get married. Before their wedding the girl went to her fiancé and said, "I love you, and I cannot imagine us ever wanting to be apart. But promise me, if such a day should come, and if I ever have to return to my parents' house, you will allow me to carry away the one thing that has become most precious to me."

The young man laughed and thought that her request was odd, especially since they had little money and very few possessions, but he saw that she was serious, and he agreed to put his promise in writing and sign it. Then they were married and began their life together.

Over the years, the couple worked very hard. They saved money, bought a nice house, and filled the house with many fine possessions. As time passed, they become rather rich and influential.

Then one afternoon, in preparation for a gathering at their house, they had a terrible argument over something unimportant. They both got emotional and said things that they regretted. "You only care about yourself and money!"

shouted the husband, as the argument escalated. "You don't care about me anymore. There is no reason for us to stay married!"

The wife was stunned by his words. For a while she was silent, and then she said, "All right, I will go. But let us stay together this evening for our party, so as not to upset our friends. I will leave when the evening is done."

The husband agreed, and they did their best to keep up appearances. As the evening went on, the wife made sure that her husband's wine glass was always full, and that he drank even more after dinner. When their guests began to leave, the husband fell asleep in the living room in a chair in front of the fireplace.

The wife said good night to the guests. Then she arranged to have her husband carried quietly to her parents' house, where he was laid in a bed. When he awakened the next morning, he was confused and asked, "Where am I? What happened?"

His wife was sitting next to the bed. She answered, "My dear, do you remember that you promised me that if we ever parted, I would be allowed to carry away the thing that had become most precious to me? Well, you are the most precious thing in the world to me, and that is why you are here. I love you more than ever, and I do not want us to part."

The husband realized how foolish he had been. He embraced his wife, and they vowed to always remember how much they meant to each other, and how their lives had been so richly blessed.

The best wealth is health.
Welsh Proverb

Nature will not give you a second life wherein
to atone for the omissions of this.
Thomas Jefferson

Nothing is to be more highly prized than the value of each day.
Goethe

Celebrate each new day with a good action, a good deed.
Leo Tolstoy

If we have not peace within ourselves,
it is vain to seek it from other sources.
La Rochefoucauld

47
BELIEVE IN MIRACLES—BECAUSE YOU ARE ONE

To me, every hour of the day and night
is an unspeakably perfect miracle.
Walt Whitman

"I have not the shadow of a doubt," said Mahatma Gandhi, "that any man or woman can achieve what I have if he or she would make the same effort and cultivate the same hope and faith. . . . I know that I have still before me a difficult path to traverse."

At first glance, Gandhi's statement may seem a bit optimistic. Very few actually succeed in matching the strength, discipline, and self-sacrifice of the physically unimposing man from India, the man who, more than anyone else at the time, shaped the events of one of the world's largest nations by insisting on the freedom and dignity of his people. He was willing to suffer (he spent a great deal of his life in prison) and even die (he fasted a total of sixteen times, sometimes to the threshold of death) in order to peacefully effect change and win victory for his fellow Indians. As Einstein eulogized Gandhi after his tragic assassination, "Generations to come, it may be, will scarce believe that such a one as this ever in flesh and blood walked upon this earth."

Nonetheless, Gandhi is correct in asserting that all of us, even though we may often fall short, have the potential to live great and fulfilling lives. It is largely a question of the effort we make, of the intensity of our desire to give something back for the miracle of our existence.

The path we must traverse, however, is indeed a difficult one. We are marvelously complex creatures with many conflicting desires and impulses. To begin with, we are part of the natural world in which one individual or species survives and prospers often at the expense of another (even by eating that other), in a cruel and intricate contest of strength and adaptability. At the same time, we humans are gifted with a remarkable consciousness of ourselves and of life that, with our unique capacity for reason, allows us to realize that cooperation can be our greatest strength and compassion our greatest salvation. Thus have arisen culture and civilization.

Each of us has the power to shape the course of his or her life and destiny to a significant degree. We can yield to our selfish and greedy impulses, which seem to come naturally, or we can walk a different path, following the dictates of our conscience, making our lives a service to our fellow human beings, thereby fulfilling the part of ourselves that is highest, most noble, and most uniquely human. Like a composer, we can, with passion tempered by discipline, make beautiful music from the cacophony of our desires and impulses; like a master artist, we can paint a beautiful portrait from the colorful pallet of our motives and aspirations. How seriously we take this task will determine whether we make of our lives masterpieces worthy of admiration and remembrance or botched and unfinished works that are unworthy of our potential.

That our commitment to serve affects the course of our lives has been a lesson of many of the world's great religions. "Give and it shall be given to you, good measure, pressed down, and shaken together, and running over," said Jesus. In the Torah it is written, "Whatsoever a man soweth, that shall he also reap." In the Talmud, it is said that "according to the measure that one metes out to others, so is it meted out to him." In Buddhism and Hinduism, we encounter the complex doctrine of Karma, which teaches that this world is a sort of spiritual school and testing ground where, in a procession of lives, we are rewarded and punished for our actions and where, in serving God and our fellow man, we can evolve to a higher, more enlightened and ultimately blissful state.

These religions are mostly concerned with our spiritual and psychological well-being. However, the idea that what we give in life determines what we receive has been given a more worldly and materialistic interpretation by others. Ralph Waldo Emerson stated, "If you love and serve men, you cannot, by any hiding or stratagem, escape remuneration." Elsewhere he wrote, "Life is a perpetual instruction in cause and effect. . . . The nature and soul of things takes on itself the guarantee of the fulfillment of every contract, so that honest service cannot come to a loss."

Emerson was perhaps influenced by the Newtonian perspective of a balanced and orderly world that prevailed in his day. Every action, said Newton, produces an equal and opposing reaction, every cause produces its commensurate effect. Newton derived this law to apply to physical phenomena that could be observed, quantified, and understood. Emerson, however, took the idea of cause and effect one step further and applied it to human behavior and relations, where it also seemed valid. If you work hard and provide excellent and honest service, then you must sooner or later be compensated for this service. The value will be recognized and rewarded; the cause creates the effect. Conversely, if you are dishonest, if you cheat someone or provide inferior service, then in time the truth will catch up and you will receive your fair and equal punishment. Such is the nature of things.

But is this true? Do we live in a just and orderly world where people always get what they deserve? It is comforting to think that we do; however, unless our rewards and punishment are carried out on a spiritual or psychological level that is difficult for us to understand or assess, experience seems to prove otherwise. All too often the seeds we sow and nurture to fruition get swept away by flood, eaten by locusts, or ravaged by drought. We may work very hard, produce superior results, be honest and sincere, yet the world does not beat a path to our door. Circumstances beyond our control—perhaps a malevolent employer, an unreceptive public, or the vicissitudes of the marketplace—prevent us from getting back what we feel is materially (or even immaterially, in terms of prestige or recognition) our just reward. Worse yet, any of us may fall victim to senseless tragedy and suffering—an act of nature, perhaps—that cuts our life short or otherwise prevents us from enjoying material success.

We don't always seem to live in a perfectly just and orderly world, at least not one that we are capable of understanding. Thus, while there is truth to what Emerson says about our actions and service shaping the material quality of our lives, this is not a position that can be defended too dogmatically. Interestingly, contemporary physicists have come to recognize something called the Uncertainty Principle. According to it, a given cause does not necessarily produce a consistent and predictable effect, and there is a significant variation in the empirical results we get from observing certain phenomena, caused in part by the unavoidable subjectivity of the human measuring these phenomena. In fact, at times something quite out of the ordinary can happen, as if fundamental particles enjoy a free will of their own. But the varying results tend to average out, a pattern emerges, and we can make reasonable estimates of the outcome of certain experiments and phenomena.

The Uncertainty Principle seems to be characteristic of our experiences in life, too. Our actions do not always produce commensurate effects. Sometimes we are rewarded materially for what we give; sometimes we are not. Sometimes something totally unpredictable and unfair happens. But over time, and up to our death (which seems a rather extreme effect suffered by us all), the ups and downs in life do tend to average out, a pattern emerges, and what we give can to a significant degree determine what we receive.

Everything is God's to give and to take away,
so share what you've been given, and that includes yourself.
Mother Teresa

When we do the best we can,
we never know what miracle is wrought in our life,
or in the life of another.
Helen Keller

Not one of us knows what effect his life produces,
and what he gives to others;
that is hidden from us and must remain so,
though we are often allowed
to see some little fraction of it, so that we may not lose courage.
Albert Schweitzer

We can be thankful to a friend for a few acres or for a little money;
yet for the freedom and command of the whole earth and for the
great benefits of our being, our life, health, and reason,
we look at ourselves as under no obligation.
Seneca

No one is useless in this world
who lightens the burden of it for anyone else.
Charles Dickens

48
FULFILL YOUR HIGHEST DESTINY

Die when I may, I want it said of me by those who knew me best,
that I always plucked a thistle and planted a flower
where I thought a flower would grow.
Abraham Lincoln

"One of the signs of passing youth," wrote Virginia Woolf, "is the birth of a sense of fellowship with other human beings as we take our place among them." Indeed, our personal existence is intricately connected and intertwined with that of others; those of us who guard the flame of life today are children of the past, parents of the future. It is at once both thrilling and sobering to know that our actions and deeds, the way in which we choose to live, have an effect on those around us, and that these people in turn have an effect on others, and so on, in an endless chain of mutual influence and dependency. Each of us helps shape our immediate world. Together we shape the future of humankind.

In the Talmud there is a parable about a traveler who comes upon an old man planting a carob tree. "When will the tree bear fruit?" asks the traveler. "Oh, perhaps in seventy years," replies the old man. "Do you expect to live to eat the fruit of that tree?" "No," says the old man, "but I didn't find the world desolate when I entered it, and as my fathers and mothers planted for me before I was born, so do I plant for those who come after me."

There is a valuable lesson in this parable: each of us who chooses to live has a responsibility to life. Not only are we indebted to those who have gone before us for their good deeds and travails, but we are also each indebted for the gift of life, which we know is something precious and magnificent beyond our comprehension. The minutes and seconds of our existence are more precious than any fortune in currency or gold, each day more valuable than any parcel of land (how can we repay God for even one breath?). It is through giving, through trying our best to do what we believe is God's will for our life, and through acting with gratitude and with what Schweitzer called *reverence for life,* that we fulfill our greatest potential as human beings.

It has long been a problem in religion, and has been considered by some an argument against religious faith, that there cannot be an all-powerful and compassionate God who allows suffering. If He is compassionate and does not put an end to the pain in this world, then He must not be omnipotent. If He is omnipotent and does not eradicate suffering, then He must not be compassionate.

This is a difficult problem, to be sure. But perhaps God has given each of us the consciousness and ability to alleviate suffering. Perhaps, like a parent who gives his children every opportunity to learn and grow, God has left it to us to fulfill our highest potential by expressing our love and creativity and by shaping the destiny of the world. "The whole world of loneliness, poverty, and pain make a mockery of what human life should be," said Bertrand Russell. And Mother Teresa observed, "Poverty is not created by God. It is created by you and me. We are responsible because we do not share."

Once a man was walking down the street in a busy city, and he saw a young child begging for food. The child was dirty and dressed in ragged clothes.

The man became angry at God and said, "How can you let such a thing happen? Why don't you do something to help this innocent child?"

Then, in the depths of his being, he heard a reply: "I did do something. I created you."

The great Jewish scholar Abraham Joshua Heschel wrote, "God's dream is to be not alone but to have humanity as a partner in the drama of continuous creation." It is certain that at almost every moment of our lives, we can do something to make this world a better and more compassionate place, whether by providing food and relief for the hungry, fighting disease, protecting the environment, helping a friend through a difficult time, or alleviating someone's loneliness with a kind word and friendly smile. This is what gives life meaning. This is the highest path we can follow. "God loves the world through us," said Mother Teresa.

Once we become conscious of life and our place in it, once we become aware of our debt to God and to each other, a part of us, the part that is highest and most uniquely human, can never be fulfilled if we turn our backs on our responsibility. Martin Luther King, Jr., once said, "As long as there is poverty in the world, I can never be rich, even if I have a billion dollars. As long as diseases are rampant and millions of people in this world cannot expect to live more than twenty-eight or thirty years, I can never be totally healthy, even if I just got a good checkup at the Mayo Clinic. I can never be what I ought to be until you are what you ought to be. This is the way the world is made. No individual or nation can stand out boasting of being independent. We are interdependent."

The hope and future of humankind lies in our becoming aware of our interdependence. Each of us is a steward of this precious thing called life. Each of us has an influence on the world; our actions set off a chain of innumerable effects. Gandhi counseled, "Be the change you want to see in the world." Socrates said, "Let him who would move the world move first himself." And Anne Frank wrote, "How wonderful it is that nobody need wait a single moment before starting to improve the world."

Teach us, Lord, to serve you as you deserve,
to give and not count the cost, to fight and not heed the wounds,
to toil and not seek for rest, to labor and not seek for any reward
save that of knowing that we do your will.

St. Ignatius Loyola

I have always held firmly to the thought that each of us
can do a little to bring some portion of misery to an end.

Albert Schweitzer

I swore never to be silent. Whenever and wherever human beings
endure suffering and humiliation, we must always take sides.
Neutrality helps the oppressor, never the tormented.
When human lives are endangered, when human dignity
is in jeopardy . . . that place must—at that moment—
become the center of the universe.

Elie Wiesel

The great enemy is indifference.

Albert Schweitzer

Injustice anywhere is a threat to justice everywhere.

Martin Luther King, Jr.

49
LEAVING THE WORLD A BETTER PLACE

Don't postpone a good deed.

Irish Proverb

nce an expert on Jewish law asked Jesus, "Teacher, what must I do to inherit eternal life?"

Jesus answered with a question of his own: "What is written in the law? How do you interpret it?"

To which the man replied: "'Love the Lord your God with all your heart, with all your mind, with all your strength,' and 'Love your neighbor as yourself.'"

"That's right," said Jesus. "If you do this you will live."

But then the man pressed Jesus for a more detailed answer, perhaps hoping to engage him in a theological debate. "And who is my neighbor?" he asked.

Jesus responded with what is probably his most famous parable, that of the Good Samaritan. "It happened that a man was going down from Jerusalem to Jericho," he said, "and he was attacked by some robbers, who beat him and stripped him of his clothes, leaving him for dead. A priest happened to come upon the injured man, and he passed by on the other side of the road. So, too, did a Levite. But then a Samaritan came upon the injured man, and when he saw him, he took pity on him. He dressed and bandaged the man's wounds, put him on the back of his donkey, and took him to an inn where he could rest and recover. He gave the innkeeper two silver coins and said, 'Please look after this man, and when I come back this way, I will come by and reimburse you for any extra expense you may have.'"

After painting this word picture and setting the stage, Jesus asked, "Which of these three men do you think was a good neighbor to the man who was beaten by the robbers?"

The expert in the law answered, "The one who had mercy on him."

"Then go and do likewise," Jesus said.

In his collection of sermons, *Strength to Love,* Martin Luther King, Jr., points out that three things distinguished the behavior of the Samaritan, making him "the conscience of mankind." To begin with, his altruism was *universal;* he did not care about the victim's race, religion, or nationality, he only cared that he was human and in need of help.

Second, the Samaritan's altruism was *dangerous.* He placed himself at risk because the road from Jerusalem to Jericho was notorious for robbers and thieves. It twisted and turned for twenty miles through the mountains, and there were many places where one could be ambushed or attacked. In fact, the wounded man himself could have been a "faker," observes King, wishing to "draw passing travelers to his side for quick and easy seizure." This is probably why the priest and the Levite didn't stop to help the wounded man: They were afraid.

Finally, the Samaritan's altruism was *excessive.* He washed and dressed the man's wounds with his own hands. Rather than calling for help, he took the man to an inn by himself and gave two pieces of silver for his lodging—the equivalent of two day's earnings for the average man, and enough to pay for about a month at an inn. He even offered to return and to give more money if the innkeeper had any extra expenses. In doing all these things, the Samaritan went far beyond what was required of him by law or almost any standard of morality. He was motivated by love.

That's all we know of the Good Samaritan. But his brief story resonates across time, prompting us to examine our own relationships and to ask, "Am I a good neighbor? Do I see all people as human beings regardless of their race, social status, or religious background? Am I willing to put myself at risk in order to do what is right? Am I willing to go the extra mile to help someone in need?"

The expert in the law asked Jesus about eternal life. More immediately, the act of giving enriches our earthly existence. Through giving, we participate in life and affect the world in which we live. We do a part of the world's work that God is calling us to do, making His love manifest by helping those whose hearts or bodies have been bloodied or bruised on their personal roads to Jericho. Such work through us can be a source of great joy and peace, making our spirit soar by connecting us to the eternal.

Each small task of everyday life
is part of the total harmony of the universe.
St. Thérèse of Lisieux

Great deeds cannot die.
They with the sun and moon renew their light forever,
blessing those that look on them.
Alfred, Lord Tennyson

The sole meaning of life is to serve humanity.
Leo Tolstoy

Do all the good you can,
By all the means you can,
In all the ways you can,
In all the places you can,
At all the times you can,
To all the people you can,
As long as you can.
John Wesley

The tragedy of life is what dies inside a person while he lives—
the death of genuine feeling, the death of inspired response,
the death of awareness that makes it possible
to feel the pain or the glory of others in oneself.
Norman Cousins

50
THE GOLDEN RULE OF SUCCESS

The highest wisdom is kindness.
The Talmud

What can you do to fulfill your responsibility to life, to make your existence deeper, more fulfilling and more meaningful? To begin with you can make your work, whatever it is that you do, a gift to the world. You don't have to be a Gandhi, a Mozart, a Socrates, or an Einstein to make a difference in the world, to live a significant life. Whatever you do, whether you are a parent, a doctor, a mechanic, a businessperson, an artist, or a politician, you can make your work an expression of your highest ideal, of your love for others, for God, and for life.

But giving goes beyond our work, as we have seen. It is the way we express ourselves, the way we relate to the world around us. Much of the teaching and wisdom of the world's great religions can be summed up in the maxim to act toward others as we would like them to act toward us. All the rest is commentary, it says in the Talmud. Indeed, it is in following this Golden Rule, in habitually expressing our love and kindness to those closest in our lives, in helping a stranger in need, in treating others the way we would want to be treated if we were in their place, that we actually break free from the limits of our personal concerns and expand to the broader interests of life and of humanity. Giving is transcendental.

Sometimes we turn from this Golden Rule of success, ignoring the dictates of our conscience and rationalizing that others, for whatever reason, are unworthy to receive what we have to give. In so doing, we deprive ourselves of life's most fulfilling experience and we deprive the world of our unique and special gift. We forget that the borders that separate us are ultimately arbitrary, that beyond our age and the color of our skin, beyond our faith in different religions and creeds, lie human beings who feel and suffer, human beings with the potential to do good things with their lives—although perhaps their dreams of doing so have been forgotten or set aside. Each is a remarkable creation; each, on some level and in some measure, deserves our love and respect; each is our neighbor on this small planet.

According to a Hasidic tale, a rabbi once asked his students how they could tell when the night had ended and the day had begun.

One of the students answered, "Is it when you can see an animal in the distance and know whether it is a lamb or a wolf?"

"That is a good answer," said the holy man, "but no."

"Is it when you can see a tree in the distance and know whether it is an olive tree or a fig tree?" asked a second student.

"No, that's not the right answer either," said the rabbi.

"Then please, tell us," the students said. "We do not know."

"When you can look into the eyes of any man or woman and see a brother or a sister, then you will know that it is the morning. If you cannot see this, then it is still the night."

Mother Teresa's entire ministry has been based on seeing people as brothers and sisters in God, on seeing the divinity in her fellow human beings. "I do it because I love God," she said. "I know that whatever I do for my brothers it is as if I did it for Him." She explains that when she and the Missionaries of Charity care for the dying and destitute, they believe that they are directly caring for Jesus himself, who said, "For I was hungry and you gave me food, I was thirsty and you gave me drink, I was a stranger and you welcomed me, I was naked and you clothed me, I was sick and you visited me, I was in prison and you came to me. . . . As you did to one of the least of these my brothers, you did also to me." This enables them lovingly to do work from which others would flee; this elevates their daily activities from thankless, grueling, menial tasks to beautiful acts of devotion.

I once had the privilege of spending some time in Calcutta, working at Mother Teresa's Home for the Destitute and Dying. There I experienced firsthand the difficulty of the work of caring for people whom nobody else would take, people with communicable diseases whom others avoid on the streets, cleaning them, dressing them, feeding them, helping them to make peace with God and to die a dignified death, surrounded by love. On one occasion, a man was brought in on a stretcher and the flesh on his lower legs had somehow been eaten away by rats and insects, exposing the bones on both legs. Some flesh remained, and this was swarming with maggots, which the Missionaries of Charity removed with patience and love. The smell, and the man's confusion and agony, were almost unbearable. I was reminded of a story: A western visitor once said to Mother Teresa, "I would not do such work even for a million dollars." "Neither would I," she replied, but I would gladly do it for God."

Hopefully most of us will never encounter such physical suffering, but we will certainly encounter people who are suffering spiritually and emotionally. "There are other kinds of worms that gnaw at people's hearts," said Mother Teresa. And, "Loneliness and the feeling of being unwanted is the most terrible poverty." Such a suffering person might be in our own neighborhood, office, or school—perhaps even in our own family. In reaching out to this person, we can know that we are also reaching out to God, and He to us in a mysterious way. Our lives will be filled with a "peace which passeth all understanding," a success beyond measure.

But what if, fatigued by problems and worries of our own, we simply do not feel love in our hearts and are not moved to give? C. S. Lewis offers some wonderful advice: "Do not waste time bothering whether you 'love' your neighbor," he says "Act as if you did." When we do this, we discover one of life's great secrets: "When you are behaving as if you love someone, you will presently come to love him," Lewis observes.

Tragically, however, the reverse can also be true. In the years leading up to World War II, Lewis points out, "The Germans perhaps at first ill-treated the Jews because they hated them: afterwards, they hated them more because they had ill-treated them. The more cruel you are, the more you hate; and the more you hate, the more cruel you become—and so on in a vicious circle forever. Good and evil both increase at compound interest."

Goodness, therefore, is a choice, sometimes a difficult choice; the Golden Rule is a way of being and the great imperative of our day. The issue of how we can best live, of what we should do with our brief and invaluable existence, is more than just an intellectual game; it is even more than a question of how we can feel most happy and successful. It is now a matter of survival. We live in a perilous age; our remarkable species has, in our selfish quest for power and riches, brought the world to the brink of destruction. In so many ways we have fallen tragically short of our ideals, of what life could be. But at times we have also displayed our capacity for love, compassion, and excellence. These actions hold the key to our survival and well-being. The choice is ours. You take part in this choice in the life you decide to live.

Judaism

What is hateful to you, do not to your fellow man.
That is the entire law; all the rest is commentary.

The Talmud

Christianity

Do unto others as you would have them do unto you.

Luke 6:31

Islam

None of you has faith unless he loves for his brother
what he loves for himself.

Hadith (Bukhari) 2:6

Buddhism

Hurt not others in ways that you would find hurtful.

Udana Varga

Hinduism

This is the sum of duty: Do naught unto others which would cause you pain if done to you.

The Mahabharata

Confucianism

"Is there one word that will keep us
on the path to the end of our days?"
"Yes, Reciprocity.
What you do not wish yourself, do not unto others."

The Analects

Other Books by Michael Lynberg

The Gift of Giving

The Path with Heart

50 Simple Things You Can Do to Save Your Life
(coauthored by the UCLA School of Public Health)

Winning! Great Coaches and Athletes Share Their Secrets of Success

A Wealth of Wisdom: Handy Lessons on Business and Life from Around the World

Meow Te Ching: The Way to Contentment, Serenity, and Getting What You Want
(written under the pseudonym Michael Kent)

The Story of the Other Wise Man
(by Henry Van Dyke, retold by Michael Lynberg)